"Your lovemaking technique is so superb, Damion, that I'd like to jot down a few notes for the research paper I'm working on."

"You want to take *notes?*" he asked. *"Now?"*

"It would be tremendously helpful if you could kiss me again, but sort of take the kiss step by step. You have a unique way of placing your hands that makes it very comfortable for the woman."

"Comfortable!" he exclaimed.

"Well, yes. When you started to kiss me I really felt able to relax and enjoy myself."

Damion poured himself another brandy. "My dear Sandi," he murmured. "How expertly you manage to cut a man down to size! Comfort, you know, isn't exactly what most of us superstuds are aiming for when we take a woman into our arms."

For a moment his eyes seemed oddly desolate. "You may find this hard to accept, Sandi, but intense mutual pleasure was more what I had in mind..."

Other Second Chance at Love books by
Jasmine Craig

Jasmine Craig was born in Wales, worked in the British Foreign Office in Rio de Janeiro, Brazil, and is now married and the mother of four children. Her family has lived in nine places around the world in the last sixteen years. She started writing because it was a career she could pursue anywhere.

Dear Reader:

The lazy days of summer are here, a perfect time to enjoy July's SECOND CHANCE AT LOVE romances.

In *Master Touch* (#274) Jasmine Craig reintroduces Hollywood idol Damion Tanner, who you'll remember as Lynn Frampton's boss in *Dear Adam* (#243). Damion *looks* like a typical devastating womanizer, but inside he's a man of intriguing depth, complexity, and contradictory impulses. He dislikes Alessandra Hawkins on sight, but can't resist pursuing her. Alessandra is thoroughly disdainful of Damion, and equally smitten. You'll love reading how these two marvelously antagonistic characters walk backward into love — resisting all the way!

In *Night of a Thousand Stars* (#275) Petra Diamond takes you where no couple has gone before — to sex in space! Astronaut Jennie Jacobs and ace pilot Dean Bradshaw have *all* the "right stuff" for such an experiment, but they've had little time to explore their more tender feelings. Suddenly their emotions catch up with them, making their coming together a bristly, challenging proposition. Petra Diamond handles their love story with sensitive realism, making *Night of a Thousand Stars* out of this world.

Laine Allen, an exciting newcomer, turns romance stereotypes on their heads in *Undercover Kisses* (#276). Every time private eye Katrina Langley asks herself, "How wrong could a woman be about a man," ultra-manly Moss Adams suggests the answer: "Very wrong!" Every time Kat thinks they're evenly matched, Moss cheerfully knocks her off balance. Moss's intelligent deviltry and Kat's swift-witted ripostes will keep you chuckling as you discover the secrets they keep from each other, while unraveling a most perplexing intrigue.

SECOND CHANCE AT LOVE is pleased to introduce another new writer — Elizabeth Henry, author of *Man Trouble* (#277). Like other heroines you've met, Marcy has a low opinion of men — especially Rick Davenport, who climbs through her bedroom window after midnight and challenges her to all sorts of fun and games. But no other heroine must contend with an alter ego called Nosy, who butts in with unasked-for advice. Nonstop banter makes *Man Trouble* as light, crunchy, and fun to consume as popcorn.

In *Suddenly That Summer* (#278) by Jennifer Rose, Carrie Delaney's so fed up with the dating game that she spends a week at a tacky singles resort, determined to find a husband. But she's so busy participating in the toga party, forest scavenger hunt, and after-dark skinny dip that she refuses to recognize the man of her dreams — even when he insists he's "it"! Thank goodness James Luddington has the cleverness and persistence to win Carrie by fair means or foul. Finding a mate has never been so confusing — or so much fun!

In *Sweet Enchantment* (#279), Diana Mars employs warmth and skill to convey the joys and heartaches of combining two families into one through a new marriage. Pamela Shaw, whom you know as Barrett Shaw's sister-in-law in *Sweet Trespass* (#182), has to deal with her son's antagonism toward her new love, Grady Talliver, *and* with Grady's four young sons. But lizards in the bathroom, a bed sprayed with perfume, and a chamber of horrors in the attic don't ruffle our heroine, who more than adequately turns the tables on her little darlings. *Sweet Enchantment* is a story many of you will identify with — and all of you will enjoy.

Have fun!

Ellen Edwards

Ellen Edwards, Senior Editor
SECOND CHANCE AT LOVE
The Berkley Publishing Group
200 Madison Avenue
New York, N.Y. 10016

Second Chance at Love

MASTER TOUCH

JASMINE CRAIG

**SECOND CHANCE AT LOVE
BOOK**

MASTER TOUCH

Requests for permission to make copies of any part of the work should be mailed to: Permissions, Second Chance at Love, The Berkley Publishing Group, 200 Madison Avenue, New York, NY 10016.

First edition published July 1985

First printing

"Second Chance at Love" and the butterfly emblem are trademarks belonging to Jove Publications, Inc.

Printed in the United States of America

Second Chance at Love books are published by
The Berkley Publishing Group
200 Madison Avenue, New York, NY 10016

*For Malcolm
in exchange for one diamond necklace
and a set of flannel sheets
with love*

Chapter One

GABRIELLA BARINI GAVE a strangled gasp, and sank with consummate grace onto the antique sofa that stood in a corner of her bedroom. She rested her head against an embroidered pillow and gazed pitifully at the slender young woman who waited impassively in the center of the room.

"You will be the death of me!" she announced in throbbing tones. "You are my daughter, but you send me to my doom!"

Sandi counted silently to ten. "On the contrary," she replied with careful calm. "I'm simply trying to save you a great deal of unnecessary pain. You need an operation, Mother, and your doctor has said you need it soon."

With the dramatic flair acquired during twenty years as a Hollywood superstar, Gabriella clasped her hand to her forehead and moaned. "You know I cannot tolerate any more of this talk about doctors and hospitals. Do not mention those horrible words to me. *Dio mio,* Sandi, but you are a cruel daughter."

1

Sandi counted silently to twenty and breathed deeply before saying, "Mother, you have an inflamed gallbladder, and your doctor has diagnosed the presence of almost a dozen gallstones. Those stones have to come out."

"You have no delicacy of soul." Gabriella shuddered. "How can you keep saying those ugly words? Gallstones! An inflamed gallbladder! They sound like something that grows inside a pig. How in the world am I to convince the media that gallstones are glamorous?"

"I have no idea. But then, I can't think of anything less important than what you tell the media. The fact is, Mother, that you're in acute pain. Next month you're scheduled to start work in California on a new movie, and unless you have those gallstones removed, you won't be able to fulfill the terms of your contract. It's obvious that you need an operation. And since you always say that you prefer American doctors, I've made arrangements for you to enter the Medical Center in Los Angeles next week. There is nothing else to discuss."

Gabriella gave another pitiful groan. "I do not know how I managed to produce a child who is so horribly practical." She stroked the opulent folds of her blue satin robe and stared in bewilderment at her daughter's neat beige linen suit.

"It is amazing, but you even *look* practical. How can that be? Certainly you cannot have acquired your character or your attitudes from me, so they must have come from your father. Yes, I am sure it is all Richard's fault. His genes are terrible, you know. Did I tell you that his father was a tax accountant?"

Sandi smiled wryly. "Yes, you've often mentioned that fact. But I'm sure Dad would be the first person to disclaim all responsibility for the way I've turned out. Believe me, Mother, accountant's genes or not, he finds me every bit as incomprehensible as you do."

Gabriella gazed thoughtfully at her daughter. "You could be beautiful, you know, if you only tried just a little. In fact, I sometimes think you have to try quite hard *not* to be beautiful. What you really need, Sandi, is a man. A real man. If you fell in love, you might eventually become quite human."

Sandi walked over to the elegant voile-draped windows, keeping her back toward her mother. She clasped her shaking hands tightly in front of her.

"What do you want me to do?" she asked with false lightness. "Change lovers every month just to prove that my hormones function normally?"

"It would be a step in the right direction, perhaps. But what you really need is a lover who will sweep you off your feet. Just once I would like to see you so much in love that you forget to be rational."

A trace of exasperated laughter tinged Sandi's reply. "Rationality isn't necessarily a crime, Mother. In some families it's even considered a virtue."

"When you were seven years old, you already had more common sense than your father and I put together." Gabriella's tone clearly indicated that she wasn't paying her daughter a compliment.

"Somebody in our household had to keep calm," Sandi said quietly.

"Was it calmness that caused you to become engaged to Jim whatever-his-name-was? The man was a walking psychology textbook, not a lover! No wonder you buy beige linen suits and wear your hair in a bun!"

Sandi swallowed hard over the lump in her throat. "My engagement to Jim ended nearly two years ago."

"And since then you've done your best to pretend you're a nun!"

Sandi swung around, a warm smile softening the classic beauty of her features. "I don't think many nuns would be suited to my profession, Mother. Sometimes you forget that I know more about human sexuality than you do."

Gabriella snorted. "The technical terms, perhaps. You

know nothing of the blissful ecstasy of the emotions, the delicious agony of unrequited love."

"On the contrary, Mother, my clients tell me about it all the time. Look, I'm not going to let you change the subject. We're supposed to be talking about you, not about the inadequacies of my love life. Please be reasonable for once. Yesterday you were in so much pain that you couldn't get out of bed. Why won't you admit that you need an operation?"

Two sparkling tears rolled down Gabriella's exquisite pink and white cheeks. "Hospitals are dreadful places, and I am not sick, except maybe a very little. I do not want those dreadful doctors to slice into my heart."

Sandi started to point out that the removal of a few gallstones didn't require a single incision anywhere near the heart, but she soon saw that Gabriella wasn't listening. Sandi crossed the room and stood beside the sofa, frustration giving unusual vehemence to her manner.

"Mother, you summoned me to Rome with a frantic phone call in the middle of the night. You said you wanted my help. Well, I've been here for more than a week, but you won't let me help you, and I can't afford to stay away from work any longer. There are a lot of people back home in Los Angeles who depend on me, and I have to think of my responsibilities to them as well as my duty to you. I'm booked on a flight to L.A. tomorrow. Please come with me. You know it would be the sensible thing to do."

"You ask the impossible!" Gabriella rose from the sofa and flung her arms wide. "You have never understood my sensitive, artistic soul. Never!"

"I guess not. I'm sorry, Mother, but I don't understand why having an artistic soul means that you must suffer agonies with gallstones instead of allowing a surgeon to remove them."

"If you were an artist, you would understand," Gabriella said darkly.

"No doubt." Sandi's voice was dry. She sighed. She and her mother had played variations on this scene every day for the past week, and she finally admitted she was achieving nothing. It would probably be best to return to the States and request her father's help. Gabriella Barini and Richard Hawkins had been divorced for more than twenty years, but Richard retained more influence over his ex-wife than any of her recent lovers. If her father was willing to tear himself away from work on his latest movie, he could persuade Gabriella to have the necessary surgery. The sooner she flew back to Los Angeles, Sandi decided, the better.

Her mind made up, she walked briskly toward the bedroom door. "Mother, I mean it this time. I'm leaving for the airport at ten tomorrow morning. Shall I wake you up to say good-bye?"

Gabriella avoided her daughter's eyes. "If you wish."

Sandi gripped the door handle so tightly that her fingers hurt, but her face betrayed none of her inner tension.

"Yes, of course I would like to say good-bye, Mother. I'll see you tomorrow, then. Good night, sleep well."

Gabriella did not reply, and after waiting for several seconds in hopeful silence, Sandi left the bedroom, closing the door softly behind her.

Chapter Two

THE DOROTHY CHANDLER PAVILION of the Los Angeles Music Center was crowded to its elegant rafters. Whichever way the television cameras turned, they recorded tightly packed rows of women glittering in sequins and diamonds, and men who almost crackled in their starched evening shirts and sober black jackets.

Despite its elegant appearance, the Pavilion was hot, and Damion Tanner stirred uncomfortably in his seat. True to form, the Academy Awards ceremony was running at least an hour behind schedule.

Damion loosened his collar, then brought his wandering attention back to the podium, where the master of ceremonies was wisecracking his way to the grand finale, the presentation of the Academy Award for this year's Best Actor. The MC's manner appeared easygoing, but Damion recognized the skill with which he was building audience suspense. He watched the performance with the detached, critical assessment of one professional ad-

7

miring another. He noted the perfect timing with which
the MC slipped in one of his quick witticisms and listened
as the audience, all three thousand of them, laughed
appreciatively.

Damion smiled, too, although he hadn't heard a word
the man had said. The professional, analytical part of his
brain was still working, but the rest of his mind seemed
to have closed down until there was nothing left except
his almost obsessive need to appear unconcerned.

His date, whose name he had momentarily forgotten,
snuggled even closer to his side, and he patted her hand
with absentminded reassurance. She was a stunningly
beautiful young woman, her delectable body sheathed in
a silver lamé gown. The studio had obviously chosen her
with considerable care, he thought cynically, since her
pale blond coloring set off his black hair and brilliant
blue eyes to perfection.

He was normally good at remembering people's
names—it was a talent that had stood him in good stead
with journalists and critics—and his mental blank on this
occasion indicated just how much effort it was costing
him to maintain his appearance of sophisticated calm.

Glancing at his date's delicate features, he saw that
her makeup was skillfully applied to make her look good
under the glaring televisions lights. He reflected without
rancor that it was probably almost as important to her
as it was to him that he win the award for Best Actor.
The studio had no doubt promised to arrange at least
one "in depth" television interview for her if Damion
Tanner won—her first big chance to appear in front of
a nationwide TV audience.

She would pretend she was Damion's lover, of course,
and during the interview would dutifully spill out whatever exotic line the publicity department had dreamed
up about their nonexistent relationship. More than a
year ago, he had stopped worrying about such studio-
concocted lies, although he often wondered how anybody
could be gullible enough to swallow such fabrications.

Until last week, when he had finished his second movie under Richard Hawkins's direction, he had spent a minimum of ten hours a day on the set, often working eighteen hours at a stretch. Yet he was still supposed to have energy enough to bed a different woman each week. The media, he thought wryly, vastly overestimated his prowess. Many nights lately brushing his teeth had just about wiped him out.

Damion scowled. He hated what the publicity department was doing, but he accepted that it was necessary.

"What is it?" his date whispered. "Is something wrong?"

"No." He forced himself to smile. His date wasn't responsible for the idiocies of the studio publicity machine. "I just wish they'd open the damned envelope."

"The presenters are coming on stage now," she whispered. "Damion, I wish you all the luck in the world." She sounded sincere, almost wistful.

"Thanks," he replied, surprised at how controlled he managed to sound. "But the sun will still rise tomorrow if I don't make it, and whatever happens, I'll put in a good word for you with the studio."

Tiffany Brandon, the co-star of Damion's successful television series, replaced the MC on stage. As usual, Tiffany was dressed in a skintight, strapless gown, and as usual, her enormous breasts were in imminent danger of popping out of their blue satin wrapping. Her gowns always seemed to be held in place chiefly by willpower. Tonight, even the willpower seemed in short supply.

Her onstage companion was Demon Rex, America's latest singing sensation. In honor of the occasion, he had changed his trademark purple makeup to a delicate shade of blue that precisely matched the color of Tiffany's dress. Somebody should have told him, Damion thought, that blue skin looked terrible on television.

Tiffany and Rex exchanged their carefully scripted lines of banter. Tiffany, an old-timer, didn't appear in the least perturbed by the knowledge that more than a hundred million people were watching the show. But Rex was clearly awed by the occasion. He read his cue cards stiffly, and his hands shook as he picked up the thick sealed envelope.

Seeing the television cameras pan in his direction, Damion exerted every ounce of professionalism to twist the tense muscles of his face into a convincing semblance of relaxation. He knew he had no real chance of winning the award, but he was determined to lose gracefully.

He had spent a couple of hours that morning working on what he would say to the reporters and talk-show hosts after he had lost, and he was quite pleased with the witty, faintly rueful speech he had come up with. To keep his mind away from what was happening on stage, he mentally recited the first few lines of his speech, calculating how best to make them sound unrehearsed.

It was extraordinarily difficult to keep his mind preoccupied. He had been nominated for his performance in *A Dream of Darkness,* although he couldn't understand why. He had watched the completed movie only once, but that was enough to convince him he was out of the running for an award. He had seen so many faults in his performance, so many places where he had fallen short of competence—let alone perfection—that it would have been torture for him to watch the movie again. At first he'd been astonished, then incredulous, then finally embarrassed, when he'd learned that he had received one of the five coveted nominations for Best Actor. For at least a week after the initial announcement he had expected the Academy to issue a statement explaining that his nomination had been a mistake. He certainly hadn't needed Richard Hawkins, his director, to warn him that the Oscar was far beyond his grasp.

"You don't have a hope, kid," Hawkins had said. He called everybody under fifty *kid.* "But don't take it to heart. They never give the award to a first-timer. They consider a nomination honor enough."

"Richard, as far as I'm concerned, it is enough. Particularly when you realize how many great actors have been nominated without ever winning it."

"Yeah, well the fact is, you'd have a better chance if you weren't so damned good-looking and if you had played a great man from the past, or a martyr or a lunatic. The Academy has a soft spot for lunatics, but it doesn't go for social misfits who screw their way to success—not unless they're Vietnam veterans, trying to get their heads together after the trauma of war. Face it, Damion. There were too many scenes in *Darkness* when you were in bed, seducing some luscious woman, with your shoulder muscles rippling in full-color close-up."

"Damn it, Richard, there was dramatic justification for every one of those scenes, and you know it!"

"Of course, I know it. Most of the critics even recognized it. But there's no way around the fact that you have a fabulous body, Damion, and the Academy doesn't like fabulous bodies, particularly on men. The judges seem to think there's an inverse relationship between the size of your pectoral muscles and the amount of acting talent you have. And when you're classically handsome as well..."

Richard had sighed, his voice trailing off dispiritedly. "You don't have a hope, kid, although I wish to God you did. An award could easily pull in an extra five million at the box office."

A burst of tense audience laughter jerked Damion out of his reverie. He heard the rip of the envelope, and for just a moment he allowed himself the luxury of closing his eyes. To hell with the television cameras, he thought. I don't want to watch this.

"The winner of this year's Academy Award for Best Actor is Damion Tanner for his performance in *A Dream of Darkness*."

He knew he hadn't heard Tiffany's announcement correctly. Too many nights of sleepless anticipation had undoubtedly distorted his perception. With phenomenal effort he fixed his mouth into a smile and listened to the thunderous applause that rolled through the auditorium. The judges' decision was obviously popular. He wanted to look around and see who was springing up to receive the Oscar, but he was too tense to move.

His date flung her arms around his neck, and he realized that she was crying. As she kissed him, he felt her tears against his cheek, the only thing he seemed capable of feeling through the ice cold layers of his self-control. If he had been able to experience any emotion, he might have been sorry for her. She'd had so many dreams riding on his success.

"Oh, Damion, you won! I knew you deserved it. I *knew* you could do it!"

Her excited words penetrated his brain. Very cautiously he removed her arms from his neck and stood up. He looked around the crowded auditorium. Nobody else was marching toward the stage, and the applause reached a new level of enthusiastic approval as he rose to his feet. He glanced along the row of seats to the left of his date. Even as he looked, Richard Hawkins jumped to his feet, applauding wildly and shouting his congratulations.

At that moment, Damion realized that Tiffany Brandon really *had* announced his name.

He drew in a deep, shuddering breath, filling his lungs as if he were about to proclaim a Shakespearean soliloquy. Carefully, very carefully, he put one foot in front of the other and walked quickly toward the stage. There was no room in his head for any thought other than a determination not to fall flat on his face, not to make a total ass of himself. It was a relief when he found that he had reached the shallow flight of stairs leading to the stage.

Tiffany smiled as she held out his Oscar. He took it dazedly, and then, because Tiffany always expected to be kissed, automatically swept her into the sort of romantic clinch that looked loaded with passion, but actually avoided mussing her waist-length hair, or popping her bosom out of its corseted confinement. She emerged from his embrace smiling triumphantly. Then, with a rare display of tact, she hustled Demon Rex from the stage, leaving Damion alone to face the audience.

Now, when it was too late to prepare himself, he finally understood why Oscar winners made such boring speeches. He experienced a moment of blind panic as he opened his mouth to speak, not at all sure that any words would come out.

A sudden hush fell over the auditorium. "Thank you, members of the Academy," he heard himself say. "And thank you, ladies and gentlemen, for your generous applause."

He noted subconsciously that his years of training for the Broadway stage kept his voice low and powerful even in this moment of acute stress. He took another deep breath and felt a surge of relief as his tension eased slightly.

"I had a wonderful speech prepared," he said, smiling as he realized that he had survived at least two minutes without making a fool of himself. "But I wasn't expecting to win, so my speech doesn't adapt very well to the present happy occasion."

The audience laughed encouragingly, and he felt warmed by the response. A bit more of his brain came out of shock, and a few rational sentences began to form in the back of his mind.

"No actor turns in an award-winning performance by himself," he said quietly. *"A Dream of Darkness* has already won an Oscar tonight for the Best Original Screenplay. Julie Blake, who played my first love, was nominated as Best Supporting Actress, and the movie was also nominated for Cinematography and Music awards. Most of you here tonight are professionals, so you know that *A Dream of Darkness* was a team effort, and its success is due to a great many people. I would like to thank all of those people—all of the members of the team who helped to make *A Dream of Darkness* into a great movie. I'm particularly grateful to Richard Hawkins, our director. Richard took a chance on me when I was unknown in Hollywood. Over the past few months he has enabled me to catch a glimpse of what movie acting is all about. If Richard and other experienced professionals like him don't lose patience with me, I hope one day to turn in a performance that truly merits the award for Best Actor. Thank you again, all of you."

He held the golden Oscar high over his head in a traditional gesture of victory, scarcely hearing the roar of applause that greeted his departure from the stage. Feeling limp, drained to the ultimate core of his being, he almost bumped into Richard Hawkins, who was waiting in the wings.

"I knew you'd do it, kid! And it was a great speech! From the moment I saw the final cut, I knew you had the Oscar in the bag!"

"Sure." Amusement replaced some of Damion's emptiness. He thumped his director affectionately on the shoulder. "I remember exactly how certain you were, my friend. That's why I spent three hours this morning practicing how to look like a good loser."

Richard grunted, avoiding a direct reply. With the help of some security guards, he fought his way to one of the dressing rooms through a throng of backstage well-wishers. "Come on, kid. Maria Merlin's waiting. The publicity goons will all be mad as hornets if you don't hook up with her before we go on to the ball. They spent days picking her out of a photo lineup."

"Maria Merlin?"

There was a touch of wry understanding in Richard's gaze. "She's your date," he said. "The woman who came with you. The woman who's been sitting next to you all evening. The woman who can't wait to show you how wonderful she is in bed."

Damion looked down at the Oscar. Coldness hit him with the sudden force of a fist aimed at the pit of his stomach. The sensation was all the more devastating for being so unexpected and so irrational.

"Oh, yes," he said slowly. "Maria. I'd forgotten her name."

There was no time to comment further. They had arrived at the dressing room, and the hallway was mobbed by reporters, half of them thrusting microphones toward him, the other half with their pencils poised over notebooks. For a split second, Damion felt a wave of utter weariness wash over him, but it vanished as soon as a reporter asked the first question. Adrenaline pumped through him, sharpening his wit and honing his instinctive sense of the dramatic. He heard his wry, self-deprecating answers and knew he was giving a wonderful performance. He had been a professional actor for fourteen years, and it had been drummed into him from day one that nobody—no star, no director, no writer—could become a success without the support of the press corps. He had been lucky so far, he reflected. The press had always been kind to him.

It was only later, when he was shut in the blissful quiet of the limo, en route to the celebratory ball, that he had time to think. For some reason he found himself wondering why he had never once considered answering the reporters' questions honestly.

With a grim twist of his mouth, he acknowledged that honest answers might have been difficult to come by. He had been acting for so long that he had virtually forgotten what it felt like to experience a genuine firsthand emotion, something so intense that he could not immediately stop and analyze his own response. He knew exactly how an Oscar winner was supposed to behave—he'd done a brilliant job of impersonating one tonight. But he wasn't at all sure how Damion Tanner actually felt about winning an Oscar for the very first movie he'd ever appeared in. Or how he felt about the fact that his parents hadn't seen fit to use the tickets he'd sent them for the Awards ceremony.

A burst of cheering warned him that they had arrived at their destination. Maria Merlin spun around from her perch by the car window. Her eyes sparkled with excitement, and her lips quivered with moist invitation.

"Isn't it wonderful?" she whispered. "There are hundreds of people out there, and they're all waiting to see *us*. Oh, Damion, I'm so thrilled that the studio chose me to be your partner this evening. I just want you to know that anything you want me to do—anything—I'll be real happy to do it for you."

He conquered the cruel urge to tell her that what he wanted most was for her to go home. In any case, when he thought about it, he wasn't sure he wanted to be alone tonight.

He reached out and ran his hand carelessly along her bare arm, recognizing the calculated expertise of her quivering response. But he had a sudden, urgent need for the warmth of physical contact and so took her into his arms anyway, kissing her with a skillful simulation of passion. A flare of desire darkened her eyes, and he could have sworn it was genuine. She obviously hadn't been in Hollywood long, he thought cynically. Didn't she know that genuine emotion was outlawed in the movie industry?

The car came to a halt, and he drew away from their kiss, then leaned forward to brush his mouth briefly across her swollen lips. A dozen cameras flashed, but he paid no attention.

"You're just wonderful," Maria breathed. "Remember, Damion, if there's anything you want..."

"Later, babe," he said softly. "When we're alone, I'll tell you exactly what I want you to do for me."

Chapter Three

DAMION SCARCELY SPOKE to Maria again that night. He was mobbed by reporters, friends, and acquaintances right up until dawn, when Richard Hawkins turned up to rescue him.

"Time to go and get breakfast," the director said, expertly detaching Damion from a reporter and three public relations flacks. "Linda's going to make it for us."

Damion peered tipsily at the cute starlet standing at Richard's side. She was twenty-four, had blond curly hair, and was Richard's fifth or sixth wife. Nobody, including Richard, seemed to bother keeping count anymore.

Damion took another swallow of champagne. "Hi, Linda," he said, then smiled, deeply impressed by his perfect diction. He repeated "Hi, Linda," several more times just to prove he could do it, and then with a conspiratorial wink, he leaned over and kissed her.

"You have a cute nose," he said.

"So do you." Linda giggled. She wasn't a very good actress, but she was sweetly pretty and had one of the kindest hearts in California. If Richard hadn't gone through five other wives before finding her, Damion would have envied him Linda. For himself, he knew that one failed marriage was more than enough to last him a lifetime, and he had no intention of repeating the experiment, not ever.

Damion linked one arm through Richard's and the other through Linda's as they walked out of the ballroom. "I don't want to get married," he announced suddenly, thrusting his finger accusingly into Richard's chest. "There's no way I'm going to get married, and you can't make me." He gestured belligerently. "Nobody can make me."

"Take my word for it, kid, I wouldn't want you to get married. It would be lousy for your image. Stay single and the women of America will thank you."

Damion grinned. "That's all right, then. You will thank me, I will thank me, and the women of America will thank me. Sounds like a good deal. We'll tell the publicity people tomorrow, and they can make an announcement. Damion Tanner, the world's most determined bachelor, has jusht won the Oshkar and promises he will never marry." He frowned. "That doesn't sound right, Richard."

His director gave him another friendly thump. "Don't worry about it, kid. Just come with us. It's time for breakfast."

Damion obediently followed his companions into the limo and sprawled over the cushioned back seat. At some point during the journey he realized he had sobered up, and he wished he hadn't. The trend of his thoughts was not reassuring.

Why wasn't he screaming his joy from the rooftops? He'd won the Oscar—the shimmering mirage that had sustained him through fourteen years of hard slogging, including two years at the start of his career when he'd often gone to bed hungry. This was definitely not the moment to be miserable.

He watched as Linda kicked off her shoes and curled up on her husband's lap. With an intensity that surprised him Damion wished there was some woman he could hold curved against his heart, secure in the knowledge that they genuinely cared about each other.

He closed his eyes, deliberately pushing the inchoate yearning away. He knew exactly what was involved in any intimate relationship, and he wanted no part of it. His parents and his ex-wife had taught him well, and he had no intention of stepping onto the merry-go-round of intimacy ever again.

He felt his mouth curve into a wry grin as he dismissed the depressing memories. It was a good thing he didn't win Oscars very often. They seemed to make him disastrously maudlin.

Linda started to sing. In a high-pitched, soft voice, she worked her way through a repertoire of songs that would have made a linebacker blush. She was still singing, with Richard and Damion harmonizing the occasional chorus, when they arrived at the Hawkins's beachfront home.

Richard began patting his pockets, searching for the house key. With much giggling, Linda ran her hands provocatively over her husband's body. She had carried her shoes from the car and dropped them somewhere on the path, so that she was almost a foot shorter than Richard. She stood on tiptoe to place her hands on his shoulders, no longer pretending to search for the key. Richard soon abandoned entirely his halfhearted efforts to open the door.

Damion watched their kiss with good-humored resignation, then reached around them to ring the doorbell. The Hawkinses had a live-in housekeeper who was probably already awake, and Linda looked as if she could use some black coffee. He was pleased to hear the immediate sound of crisp, firm footsteps tapping on tile. Somebody was crossing the hallway and coming to let them in.

The heavy door swung open, but it was not the housekeeper who greeted them. A tall, slim young woman with dark hair and vivid green eyes stood silently in the entrance. Despite the early hour she was immaculately dressed in a tailored beige suit and a cinnamon brown silk blouse. Her feet were encased in plain high-heeled pumps, and her hair was swept up into a complicated French knot. Her makeup was minimal, but definitely there; Damion had the impression that it was designed to indicate that her outfit was complete rather than to enhance her femininity. Her cool gaze swept over him just once—comprehensively—and then she turned toward Richard and Linda. Damion, unused to being so summarily dismissed, fought back a crazy impulse to grab her face and force her to look at him properly.

She still hadn't uttered a single word, but her effect on Linda was electric.

"Sandi!" Linda gasped. "Oh, good heavens!"

She pulled herself out of her husband's arms and began to scrabble around on the patio for her missing shoes. When that quest proved unsuccessful, she fussed with the neckline of her evening gown, looking for all the world like a teenager caught making out in the back seat of her parents' car.

The woman's effect on Richard was equally dramatic.

"Oh . . . um . . . hello, Sandi," he mumbled, as he attempted to fasten the studs of his evening shirt and smooth his rumpled hair. Richard Hawkins was known throughout the movie industry for his terrifying ability to make grown men tremble, but at that moment Damion could have sworn his director was actually blushing.

The woman finally spoke. "Hello, Linda, how are you? Hello, Dad. You're looking pretty snazzy. What's the special occasion?"

Her gaze once again swept coolly over Damion before coming to rest on Richard and Linda. She smiled, a touch of tolerant affection gleaming in her green eyes.

Dad? Damion shot an astonished glance at Richard. He hadn't realized that any of the Hawkins marriages had lasted long enough to produce a child, and Richard had certainly never mentioned the existence of a daughter.

"Dad, I really need to speak with you about something," Sandi said. "I stopped by early so I could catch you before you left for the studio. I hope you don't mind."

Richard cleared his throat. "No, no, of course, I don't mind, Sandi. In fact, it's wonderful to see you, sweetheart. Just wonderful. May we come in?"

The laughter in her eyes deepened. "Dad, it's your house, not mine." She moved aside.

Richard and Linda stepped into their own elegant hallway, still looking as if they weren't sure they belonged there, and Damion followed, wondering why on earth they were both still preoccupied with futile attempts to straighten their clothes. They had obviously spent all night celebrating, but so what? It was certainly no business of Sandi's if they decided to spend a night out on the town or to indulge in a little love play on their own patio. But then, he knew from bitter experience that most women were afflicted with an obsessive need to control the lives of the men in their families. This woman was obviously no exception.

Watching her neat ankles and the sway of her wrinkle-free suit as she walked in front of him, he felt another sharp flare of resentment. He was a bit surprised at how angry her faultless rearview made him fell. Her perfect appearance inspired him with a crazy urge to ruffle her composure. He wondered how she would look with her dark hair pulled out of its smooth twist and her slim body stripped of its immaculate clothes. For some reason he found the image of a disheveled Sandi extremely erotic, but he pushed the picture out of his mind with more than a touch of impatience. Heaven knew it had been a long time since his last affair, but he must have been without sex for even longer than he'd realized if he was beginning to fantasize about this repressed stick of a woman.

They all trooped into the living area, a parquet-floored, high-beamed room with a floor-to-ceiling glass wall and a panoramic view of the ocean. Linda tossed her evening purse onto the white velvet sofa.

"I'll fix us all a pot of coffee," she said, her voice unnaturally bright.

"Would you like me to help?" Sandi asked.

"No, thank you. You . . . er . . . you stay and chat with your—um—stay and chat with Richard. You haven't seen each other for ages."

Linda escaped from the living room with a visible sigh of relief. No wonder she had sounded almost incoherent, Damion thought. He had rarely encountered a woman as off-putting as Sandi. Richard's daughter was definitely not the sort of woman you wanted around when you were less than sober.

It was her smile that got to you, he decided. That damned tolerant smile made him think of the Mother Superior at a convent, inspecting a row of scruffy children. It was enough to make a normal person wonder if he was wearing matching socks, or if his shirt was tucked into his trousers. He wondered what she did for a living. Probably a computer programmer or a high school math teacher. Definitely some rigidly conservative profession whose practitioners felt no need for human warmth or sympathy.

Richard gave his daughter an affectionate hug, from which she emerged still looking untouched by human hand. Her skin and hair shed the effects of physical contact with the ease of high-grade polyester.

"It sure is terrific to see you, sweetheart," Richard said. "But I thought you were going to stay in Italy for another week at least."

"No. I couldn't spare any more time from work."

Richard looked uncomfortable. "Oh, yes, of course. Your—um—work."

Sandi didn't reply, and with an obvious desire to change the subject, Richard clasped his daughter's shoulders. "Well, sweetheart, I'm glad you're here because I want to introduce you to a very special friend of mine. You saw his fabulous performance in *A Dream of Darkness*, but wait until you see him in the final version of *Floodtide*. He'll make your blood freeze in your veins, I swear it. Sandi, this is Damion Tanner. And Damion, this is my daughter, Alessandra Hawkins. We call her Sandi."

"Hello, Damion." If she was impressed at meeting the winner of this year's Academy Award for Best Actor, she gave no sign of it. Her green eyes met his head on, and for a split second he felt an inexplicable tightening somewhere deep in his gut. It was an extraordinary sensation, and he didn't like it one bit.

"Hello, Sandi," he said, positively dripping charm. Her response to the introduction had been so chilly that he took a perverse pleasure in making his own voice throb with warmth. "I'm delighted to meet you. It's certainly a great pleasure to meet Richard's daughter at last." He extended his hand, at the same time producing one of his most devastating smiles.

Her handshake was as brief and cool as her greeting, and her expression registered nothing more than faint amusement. Damion concluded ruefully that his Oscar-winning smile, the one guaranteed to melt the average woman's bones, had absolutely no effect on Alessandra Hawkins. Her indifference ought to have been a refreshing change after the cloying adulation he'd received in the past few hours. Instead, he felt obscurely annoyed by his failure to impress her. His slow, sensual smile was practically patented, dammit! Why didn't it work on Alessandra Hawkins?

"I apologize if my arrival here interrupted something important," Sandi said, her voice as well bred, well organized, and well modulated as the rest of her. Damion hated it. "I do hope I didn't cut short any important discussions?"

Since she had discovered all three of them singing ribald songs on the doorstep, she knew darn well they hadn't been discussing anything even marginally significant. Damion felt his body tightening in preparation for the attack.

"It's obviously been quite a while since you saw your father, whereas Richard and I see each other every day." He smiled with exaggerated courtesy. "Don't worry about it, Sandi. We can continue our discussion after you leave."

The faintest trace of color crept into her cheeks, but she gave no other sign that she was aware of his rudeness. She simply looked at Damion in assessing silence for a moment before turning to face her father.

"Dad, I have a favor to ask you, but I'll come back later. I hoped to catch you before the start of your other appointments, but I can see that my timing wasn't very good. Would this evening be a convenient time for us to talk?" For the first time Damion sensed an element of hesitation in her words. "It's about Mother," she added.

Richard, who had been dozing in an armchair, looked up quickly. "About Gabriella? Something's wrong?"

Sandi smiled with a warmth that totally transformed her face. Damion discovered that he was holding his breath and let it out sharply, turning away to stare out the window.

"Nothing that you won't be able to put right," he heard Sandi say. "Don't worry about it, Dad."

Linda entered at that moment, carrying a tray laden with a coffee pot, sugar bowl, and mugs. "Here you are, everybody. Fresh coffee!" Ingenuously, she added, "Mrs. Sanchez helped me to make it, so it's sure to be good."

Damion set the tray on the low table in front of the fireplace. Linda had taken advantage of her absence to change into a turquoise satin robe. The sophisticated style emphasized her soft, fluffy prettiness. With a shock Damion realized that she might well be a couple of years younger than Sandi. For the first time he felt a tiny glimmer of sympathy for Richard's daughter. It couldn't be easy to have a stepmother who was younger than you were, particularly when she was the fifth or sixth woman to fill that role.

Richard leaned back in his chair, stirring his coffee. "We didn't know you were home from Italy, Sandi, or we'd have sent you tickets for the show."

"The show?"

"The Academy Awards."

"Oh, Lord, how could I have forgotten? The ceremony was last night! I'm sorry, Dad, but transatlantic flights always zap me for the best part of twenty-four hours. And this time the plane left Rome so late that I missed my connection in New York and it took me nearly thirty hours to get home. I slept all day yesterday, then woke up at the crack of dawn this morning. How did the awards go? Did *A Dream of Darkness* win?"

"Two out of the five nominations." Richard's face stretched into a huge, satisfied grin. "My script won the award for Best Original Screenplay, and right at this moment you're gazing into the eyes of this year's Best Actor."

Sandi put her coffee mug down on the table. "I never gaze into men's eyes," she said composedly. She rose from her chair with the controlled grace Damion already thought of as her trademark and pressed a light kiss against her father's cheek. "Congratulations, Dad. I'm thrilled and delighted for you. No wonder you and Linda looked so happy when you arrived home!"

"We'd been drinking champagne all night long," Linda confessed.

"If you can't drink champagne when you win an Oscar, when can you?" Sandi smiled kindly at her stepmother, and Damion fought back the urge to kick her right in her patronizing fanny. He took a very large swallow of coffee. It didn't help much, and he now had a burned mouth as well.

"Congratulations to you, too, Damion," she said politely. "It's almost unheard of for an actor to win an Oscar for his first movie, but I'm sure the judges knew what they were doing."

Richard and Linda both beamed happily, but Damion had no difficulty detecting the knife blade beneath her soft words.

"Well, thank you, honey," he said, emphasizing the *honey*. Some instinct told him she would hate the casual Hollywood endearment. "But you're really too generous in your praise."

Just for a moment her gaze clashed with his, and he saw that she wasn't quite as cool as she pretended to be. Green fire shone in her eyes, and he realized with a shock that their dislike was not only irrational but also mutual.

"I wasn't generous at all," she said with deadly sweetness. "I thought you were brilliant in the role, Damion. In fact, most of the time you were so convincing that it was hard to believe you weren't simply playing yourself."

His expression hardened. "Every actor draws on personal experience in interpreting a role."

Her smile became two degrees more deadly. "I'm sure he does. And your experience certainly seems to have been exceptionally energetic, not to mention widely varied. I was deeply impressed by the range of sexual expertise you displayed, Damion."

The hero of *A Dream of Darkness* had made love to every woman he met between the ages of sixteen and sixty. The point of the movie, however, had not been to show that the hero was dynamite in the bedroom. Damion had exerted every ounce of professional skill he possessed to convey that the hero had been terrified of his own sexual inadequacy. He bit down on an angry and somewhat juvenile retort—what would be the point of trying to explain such a concept to a woman like Sandi?—but his effort at self-control was wasted. Sandi was already taking leave of her father and stepmother, explaining that she was late for work.

"I'll come with you," Damion said, rising abruptly to his feet. "My driver has to get back to the city; he can drop you off wherever you need to go."

As soon as he had spoken, he wished he could rescind the offer. What in heaven's name had prompted him to suggest spending more time with Alessandra Hawkins, nature's perfect answer to the frost-free freezer? He smiled grimly. Since winning the Oscar, he had gained several interesting insights into his own character. Until he met Alessandra Hawkins, for example, he had never realized he had some distinctly masochistic tendencies.

Sandi picked up a neat dark brown purse that matched her neat dark brown shoes. "Thank you, Damion, but I have my own car. There's no need to take your driver out of his way."

The knowledge that she had absolutely no desire to spend any more time with him made him push the issue. Her elusiveness provoked him into a ridiculous adolescent impulse to glue himself to her side.

"Then perhaps you'd be kind enough to give me a ride?" He produced one of his dazzling, little-boy-lost smiles, more to annoy her than to influence her decision. She had already shown herself to be disconcertingly impervious to his high-voltage smiles.

"Your father has to tape a television interview this morning," Damion added. "He really needs the limo. If I come with you, the studio won't have to find another driver."

He sensed the conflict between her courtesy and her personal preference, but he wasn't surprised when courtesy won out. He had the strong impression that Sandi Hawkins rarely allowed her emotions to triumph over her good manners. She smoothed a nonexistent wrinkle from her spotless skirt and walked toward the door.

"Of course. It will be my pleasure to drive you home. If you're ready then, Damion, I'd like to leave right away. My first appointment is at nine."

He quickly took his leave of Richard and Linda, then followed Sandi out to the carport. Her car was a Toyota Celica. Its dark gray interior looked as though it was vacuumed twice daily and its pale gray exterior looked so highly polished that Damion wondered if freeway dust ever dared to pollute it.

He settled into the passenger seat without looking at Sandi and stared morosely out the window, wondering what the hell he had let himself in for. Right now he could have been snoozing quietly in the back of the limo or even relaxing with Richard and Linda. The more he thought about it, the less he understood why he was sitting beside a woman he didn't like and had absolutely no desire to know any better.

He stole a glimpse at Sandi's profile. She certainly didn't look as if she was bursting to converse with him. With luck they might manage to pass the journey in total silence, which would suit him just fine. He, for one, had no intention of saying or doing anything that would provoke an interchange.

"Would you please fasten your seat belt, Damion?"

His good intentions disappeared in a flash. "Why?" he asked with heavy sarcasm. "Are you planning to crash the car?"

"No," she responded politely. She held out one half of the seat belt with the air of a kindly adult determined to deal patiently with her half-witted child. "But it's sensible to take such a simple precaution, don't you think? Who knows how everybody else will be driving this morning? They may all be feeling as hung over and grouchy as you are."

She smiled at him benevolently, and he gritted his

teeth, infuriated by her patient good humor. It had been bad enough back at the house when she had shown at least an occasional glimmer of irritation, but he couldn't stand this attitude of cheerful indifference. He sat up straighter in his seat. Scarcely a woman he'd met could resist him once he made an effort to please her. Surely Sandi would soon prove she was no exception to the rule.

He lowered his mellow voice to a husky, confiding murmur. "I really appreciate your offer to drive me home, Sandi. I hope I'm not taking you too far out of your way."

"You haven't told me yet where you want to go."

He resisted the sudden, ridiculous urge to lean across the stick shift and kiss her until the laughter in her eyes changed to a blur of passion. "To Orange Grove Boulevard," he said, keeping his voice mellow and seductive. "I have an apartment there. It's really quite comfortable for a bachelor."

"I'm sure it is," she said. "And no, you're not taking me far out of my way."

What in blazes was she smiling about now? he wondered. Silence descended, and she made no effort to break it. Damion reminded himself that he had no desire to talk to her. He closed his eyes, planning to fall sleep.

They had traveled less than a mile when his eyes opened again. "Richard never mentioned he had any children," he heard himself say, a distinct trace of belligerence in his voice. Just being near Sandi Hawkins was enough to keep his temper simmering perilously close to boiling.

"I'm twenty-eight," she said coolly, as if that explained everything.

"So?"

She shrugged. "Linda is twenty-four. Ex-wife number five has only just had her thirtieth birthday."

To any other woman, Damion would have expressed his sympathetic understanding, but Sandi didn't appear at all perturbed by the fact that her father was married to a woman thirty years younger than he was and four years younger than his daughter. She changed lanes with rapid expertise and headed for the freeway exit. She had taken the quickest route and hadn't once asked him for directions. Until this morning he hadn't known how much he disliked efficient women.

"Alessandra is a beautiful name," he said. The more impervious she seemed toward him, the more he felt compelled to exert his famous charm. "Was your mother Italian?"

"My mother is Gabriella Barini," Sandi replied, her voice matter-of-fact as she named one of the screen's most famous, and most volatile stars. Rumor had it that Gabriella on a movie set produced about equal proportions of superlative acting and mind-boggling displays of temperament.

"She was my father's first wife. They were married when she was eighteen, and I was born six months later. They were divorced before she was twenty, but my father gave Gabriella her first big chance when he cast her as the female lead in *Nighthawk*."

"I had no idea your father was once married to Gabriella Barini."

"Nothing about their relationship was in the least bit secret," Sandi said dryly. "Didn't you ever read fan magazines when you were a child?"

"No." For a moment Damion forgot how much Sandi annoyed him and simply answered her question honestly. "Most actors seem to be born knowing that they want to act. But when I was in school, acting was just about the last career I imagined myself following. I never appeared in any school plays, and I don't remember going to the movies more often than my friends." He grinned suddenly. "Then, as I got older, when I did go to the movies, I was much more interested in making out with my girl friend than watching what was happening on the big screen."

"I'm sure you were." Sandi's expression didn't change, but he detected a faint trace of genuine laughter in her voice. She turned into the tree-lined street that led to his apartment complex, a fashionable high-rise built around a fountain-filled plaza.

"A publicity handout I read said that you appeared in your first Off-Broadway production when you were nineteen," Sandi commented, slowing down to comply with the speed limit. Damion had never driven down this road at a legal speed before, and he looked at his neighborhood buildings with interest. Several of them were actually quite attractive.

"What were you doing in an Off-Broadway play at such a young age if you weren't interested in acting?" Sandi asked.

"I discovered the theater during my freshman year at college. A friend recruited me for the Drama Club, and I played the chief witch in a Halloween extravaganza. From that moment on I was hooked."

She looked directly at him for the first time since they'd entered the car. "Chief *witch?*" she queried with a tiny grin.

"Yeah, well, the producer had a somewhat flexible understanding of gender, but a keen eye for dramatic effect. He wanted a tall witch, and I was the tallest person in the Drama Club. It was the most important part in the play, and the girls were all very jealous."

She laughed softly. It was the first time he had heard her laugh, and he was amazed at how much he liked the sound.

"You're home," she said, drawing the Toyota to a smooth halt at the curb.

"Would you come in and have some coffee?" he asked.

Her silence lasted no more than a second or two.

"It's nice of you to ask, but no, thank you, Damion. I have only fifteen minutes to make my nine o'clock appointment."

He told himself he was relieved by her refusal. It had

been crazy to invite her up to his apartment when they had absolutely nothing in common. Heaven knew, it wasn't as if he found her physically attractive, and mentally she was a total turn-off.

"Well, thanks for the ride, Sandi. We should have lunch some time."

Ironic laughter gleamed in her eyes again. "Sure," she said. "Let's do that real soon, Damion."

He slammed the door of the Toyota with unnecessary violence and walked into his apartment building. It was impossible to be polite to the wretched woman, he thought angrily, delighted to know he'd seen the last of her.

He nodded to the doorman, accepting his congratulations with an absentminded smile, his thoughts still on Alessandra Hawkins.

A single *small* dose of a woman like her, he concluded, was more than enough to last any normal man for a lifetime.

Chapter Four

EARLY THE NEXT morning Sandi leaned back in the chair so that the makeup artist could smooth pancake foundation over her face. Now that she was actually at the television studios, she bitterly regretted her agreement to appear on Mark Kline's morning news show. Apart from any other consideration, she had been forced to postpone four appointments at the clinic in order to free up the necessary time, and at least one of her clients couldn't afford the postponement. He was getting married next week and needed all the help he could get.

In retrospect Sandi couldn't understand how she had come to accept the invitation. She rarely acted on impulse, which was probably lucky for everybody. Experience had proven that those rare occasions when she followed her instincts invariably resulted in disaster. Yet she had allowed an absurd, adolescent interest in Damion Tanner to overcome her common sense, the attribute she valued most highly, and agreed to appear on the Mark Kline show with Damion Tanner.

Sandi found herself thinking about yesterday morning, when she had opened the door of her father's house to find Damion leaning against one of the patio pillars. Surprisingly, his expression had seemed almost austere in that first fleeting instant, heightening the contrast between the lean, intelligent cast of his features and the sensuality of his body.

His black tie had hung loosely around his neck, and his ruffled evening shirt had been unbuttoned halfway to his waist, revealing a stretch of bronzed skin and a fascinating trace of dark chest hair. Later, when she was alone, she'd decided cynically that he must experiment in front of a full-length mirror until he got the amount of naked flesh just right—perfectly calculated to produce the maximum response from susceptible females. All the same, she had had to swallow hard and look away. It had taken all of her considerable willpower to keep her mouth from falling open.

His mocking blue gaze had drifted over her dismissively, and she had been shocked to discover that she didn't want Damion Tanner to ignore her. She wanted to rest her hand against that intriguing expanse of bare skin. She wanted to curl his dark hair around her fingers. She wanted to feel the ripple of hard muscle beneath her palms.

Sandi was bewildered by her own feelings. She had been meeting Hollywood screen idols since she was a baby, and her usual reaction hovered somewhere between faint amusement and outright boredom.

But yesterday it had taken her a full minute to gain sufficient control of herself to speak. Even now she had no real memory of what she had said, although she remembered that she had followed Damion's every movement as he walked around the living room. Face it, she thought wryly. You were transfixed by the man's blatant sexuality.

Her attraction was doubly embarrassing, not only because of her profession but also because she felt sure that Damion's animal magnetism was as phony as it appeared potent. If there was one thing her years in Hollywood had taught her, it was that nothing about the glitzy world of moviemaking was real. The more erotic Damion Tanner appeared on the screen, the more strongly she suspected that his sexual performance in real life would leave a lot to be desired.

In Sandi's experience, movie stars invariably had giant-sized egos to match their giant-sized talents. She accepted that great actors needed a strong self-image to survive the battering they took on the way to the top. But their obsession with their own careers not only made them disastrous parents, it also made them unfaithful spouses and unreliable friends. She had been thirteen years old when her father entered into his third marriage and her mother took on her seventh live-in lover. Right then, Sandi had made the decision never to get emotionally involved with an actor, and she had never regretted that decision.

Her work at the clinic gave scientific backing to her opinion that movie stars might look terrific on the silver screen, but they weren't much fun to be around when the cameras stopped rolling. Some interesting recent studies had blown away the myth that virile, aggressively masculine men made the best lovers. Several recent surveys had shown that gentle, quiet men were not only more satisfying as lovers but also more technically accomplished because they cared about their partners' satisfaction. Women might fantasize about being seized by a marauding sheikh who carried them off to his desert lair and ravished them on silken cushions. In real life they wanted a man who was kind and considerate, who would intersperse his lovemaking with tenderness and laughter—and who might even volunteer to help wash the dishes when the lovemaking was over.

"If you'll cover your eyes, Dr. Hawkins, I'll give you

a touch of hair spray," the makeup artist said. "We don't want your chignon falling down in the heat of battle."

She picked up the plastic face shield and covered her eyes.

"*Battle* is all too apt a term for what Mark Kline probably has in store for me," she commented.

The makeup man grinned consolingly. "I wouldn't worry about it, Dr. Hawkins. Mark never sets out to make people look foolish."

"That may be true," she said ruefully, "but I've watched him too many times to feel reassured. He doesn't need to set traps for people. He just chooses his guests carefully, then waits for them to make fools of each other."

"I doubt if anybody'll make a fool out of you, Dr. Hawkins. I saw you when you were on with that nasty New York talk-show host. If you can survive that, you can survive anything."

"Maybe. Personally, I'm not so sure. Mr. Tanner isn't going to like what I say about *A Dream of Darkness.*"

"I already made up Mr. Tanner," the makeup man remarked conversationally. "He's very easy to work with, not like some movie stars. You'd never know he just won the Oscar. Have you met him?"

"Just once."

"In my opinion, his performance carried that movie. I took my girl friend to one of the previews, and she scarcely spoke to me for a week after we'd seen it. She was too busy sighing over Damion Tanner." He tossed a comb into the sterilizing jar, his manner as cheerful as ever. "The next time I went into her bedroom, darned if there wasn't a giant poster of Damion hanging over the bed. Stripped to the waist and ready for action, if you know what I mean."

"Weren't you jealous?" Sandi asked, professional curiosity getting the better of her discretion.

He shrugged. "Damion Tanner's just a fantasy stuck on the wall. *I'm* real."

The makeup man was obviously well adjusted and happy with himself, Sandi concluded. She wished all her clients could enjoy the same degree of self-confidence.

He dusted powder across her nose. "There you are, Dr. Hawkins," he said, admiring his efforts. "You're all done."

"Thank you. I appreciate your help."

"My pleasure." He removed the protective cape from her shoulders with a flourish, and she stared at herself in the mirror. The brilliant lights around the glass revealed makeup that was a little heavier than usual, eyes that seemed just a tiny bit more emerald in the pale oval of her face, and cheekbones that were artfully touched with blusher. On the whole, however, she looked pretty much as she always did—aloof, reserved, and unapproachable.

She wasn't sure what made a person's face look unapproachable, but hers certainly did. When she first started doing clinical work, she had worried about her aloof appearance, but she soon discovered that her worries were unnecessary. Clients found her brisk, down-to-earth manner reassuring. In fact, the more intimate their revelations, the better they liked her faint aura of formality. Her appearance of unshockable reserve had turned out to be a professional plus instead of a minus.

The makeup man summoned a young production assistant, who helped Sandi find her way to the lounge where Mark Kline's other guests were awaiting their turn on camera. As soon as she walked into the room, she spotted Damion Tanner, and her stomach lurched slightly, even as her breathing quickened.

She noted her own reaction with determined professional detachment, realizing she was experiencing the earliest stage of sexual desire. It was caused by a straightforward biochemical reaction and had absolutely nothing to do with her real feelings for Damion Tanner. For some unknown reason her body responded violently to his pheromones. This didn't mean that they possessed a single interest or idea in common. It didn't mean that they liked each other, or that they would enjoy spending a night out together.

Sandi considered it an unfortunate truth that human beings, along with moths, mosquitoes, and miscellaneous other crawling creatures, were initially attracted to each other by a subliminal awareness of each other's scent. Since the attraction was caused by genetically endowed body chemistry, there was no way to control it. Unlike insects, however, human beings were expected to live together after the mating was over, and professional research had long since convinced Sandi that biochemical reactions made an unstable basis for a permanent relationship. In her considered opinion, the power of chemical attraction—otherwise known as sex appeal—had caused humankind a great deal of unnecessary grief over the centuries. In a better ordered universe, matters would have been arranged differently. She, for one, had no intention of allowing hormonal secretions to determine her destiny.

Telling herself firmly that she wouldn't look in Damion's direction, she went to the water cooler and drew herself a drink. There was no point in giving her overactive hormones any unnecessary assistance.

Her excellent resolution lasted approximately twenty seconds before her gaze slid back toward Damion. He was surrounded by a cluster of guests and technicians, all eager to speak with this year's winner of the Academy Award for Best Actor. He was making a marvelous job of it, she decided irritably. The studio publicity people would be proud of him.

For a while she thought she might avoid any conversation with him, but he looked up suddenly, as if sensing her disapproving scrutiny, and his bright blue eyes met hers with the impact of a bulldozer crashing into a brick wall. Then he smiled.

Her mouth went dry, her heart pounded, and her palms

became damp. The second stage of physical desire, she thought, sipping cold water and fighting to remain calm. The feeling was caused by nothing more than a dilation of blood vessels as an increased blood supply rushed to certain parts of her body.

Sandi frowned. *Nobody's* smile could possibly have such a devastating effect on her. Her pounding heart and damp palms were undoubtedly caused by nerves. After all, she didn't often appear on television.

She had just reached this happy conclusion when Damion started to walk toward her. She took one more quick look at him, then concentrated on thinking neutral thoughts.

Her body, however, wasn't interested in neutral thoughts. At this precise moment it was interested in noticing that Damion Tanner moved with the innate, sensual appeal of a stalking tiger, that he threw off pheromones at a rate sufficient to captivate the entire female population of Los Angeles.

Sandi discovered that her body was an amazingly well tuned and efficient biological instrument. It registered Damion's high level of sex appeal and reacted accordingly. It pumped extra blood, it squeezed the air out of her lungs, it melted her bones and generally prepared her for instantaneous submission. Her brain sent out a few pitiful reminders that she cordially disliked Damion Tanner and all that he stood for, but her body paid no attention to these sensible messages.

"Sandi, this is a pleasant surprise." His low, clear voice sent a shiver down her spine. The light touch of his hand against her sleeve set her pulse pounding. Sandi did her best to ignore the sensations.

"Hello, Damion, how are you?" To her relief her voice sounded pretty normal.

"Just fine, thanks. Are you here with your father? I didn't know Richard was going to be on this show. I thought he did his final stint yesterday."

"He did," she snapped. How typical of the man to

assume that she was here only in her role as Richard
Hawkins's daughter! How typically, arrogantly chauvin-
istic! And didn't he ever do up the buttons on his shirt?
All he needed was a gold pendant nestling against his
hairy chest and he'd be a walking stereotype.

She injected all the frostiness she could muster into
her voice. "Mark Kline invited me to discuss *A Dream
of Darkness* in my professional capacity."

It was infuriating to see that her frostiness merely
amused him. His eyes darkened with laughter. "Well,
that's great, honey! I didn't realize you were professionally involved in the movie industry. Do you work in
publicity?"

"No," she said, grinding her teeth to restrain herself
from telling him exactly what she thought about men
who called her *honey*. "I'm not involved in the movie
industry, except that I spend a great deal of time treating
people who are victims of the Hollywood propaganda
machine."

She was gratified to see that she had succeeded in
surprising him. He looked startled, as well he might,
although she regretted that she'd spoken so tartly. At that
moment, the production assistant warned them that their
time on the air had almost arrived, and Sandi was relieved
by the interruption.

It was out of character for her to be so churned up
over nothing. Her parents both considered her the per-
sonification of all that was calm and rational. Long before
she was old enough to attend junior high school, she had
discovered the secret of remaining cool in the midst of
emotional tempests that would have destroyed most children. Living with Gabriella Barini was pretty much like
living with a permanently erupting volcano, and Sandi
had learned early how to avoid getting burned by the
flowing lava.

She followed the production assistant, puzzled by her
reaction to Damion. She could blame body chemistry for

the sexual tension he aroused, but she had no idea what to blame for the simmering anger he provoked.

Mark Kline greeted them both with warm, courteous smiles and settled them into two comfortable chairs, one on either side of him.

"You know more or less what I'm going to ask you, Sandi, because we've already discussed it. As for you, Damion, I'm just going to ask the standard questions. How you got the part in this movie. What you felt while you were working on it. How you got along with Julie Blake, your co-star. How you feel about winning an Oscar for your first film."

"It all sounds suspiciously low-key for your program, Mark. I warn you, I'm prepared to find a few zingers tucked away in there somewhere."

Despite his words, Damion's smile was relaxed. Television, Sandi remembered, was the medium in which he had originally made his name, and he was clearly at home in the hot, pressure-filled atmosphere of the studio.

Mark's smiled widened. "I liked *A Dream of Darkness*," he said easily. "Don't worry, Damion. I'm not planning to land any low blows."

Damion's expression remained skeptical, but the producer's hand signals indicated that the commercial break was only twenty seconds away from ending, and Mark Kline turned to face the cameras. The recording light flashed on.

"Welcome back," Mark said to his unseen television audience. "I think my next two guests will be of particular interest to us all. Damion Tanner, the incandescent star of *A Dream of Darkness* and winner of this year's Academy Award for Best Actor, needs no introduction. Even if we didn't like his movie, we are all eternally grateful to him for making one of the shorter acceptance speeches on recent record."

There was a ripple of laughter from the studio audience as Mark Kline began to run through his promised

list of questions. Damion fielded them all with practiced
ease and considerable charm. Yes, he'd thoroughly enjoyed working with Richard Hawkins. Yes, Julie Blake
was a talented actress who had made his own performance look better than it actually was. Yes, he missed
working in television, but he was considering an offer
to star in a miniseries based on the life of Genghis Khan.
Yes, he'd been astonished to win an Academy Award for
his very first film. He understood that it was an almost
unheard of achievement. He was very humbled by the
honor.

Mark Kline paused to draw breath. His smile never
wavered, but a tiny pulse throbbing on his jaw alerted
Sandi to the fact that he was moving on to the attack.

"Some critics have suggested that the Academy re-
warded you more for your superlative body than for your
acting ability, Damion. How would you answer that crit-
icism?"

"First, by suggesting that critics should see the film
before they write their comments," Damion said curtly.
A Dream of Darkness tells the story of a young man
obsessed by his own sense of inferiority. He can't recognize the genuine talents that he possesses, and he uses
people—chiefly women—in a desperate attempt to make
it to the top. I don't really see what that story has to do
with the supposed attractions of my body, although naturally I'm flattered that some critics think it's so spec-
tacular. If my next film is unsuccessful, maybe I can
make a living endorsing vitamin pills."

Mark Kline interrupted a burst of friendly audience
laughter. "I take it, then, Damion, that you don't consider
yourself Hollywood's latest sex symbol?"

"I'm an actor," he said tersely. "I've just explained
that in *A Dream of Darkness* I portray a young man who
uses sex as a weapon in the battle he wages against the
world. Naturally there are several explicitly sexual scenes

in the movie. But I fail to see why those scenes turn me personally into a sex symbol. Movie critics, of all people, ought to be able to distinguish between the actor and the man."

"I'm sure we all agree with that final comment, and thank you for your frank remarks," Mark Kline said as he swiveled around to face Sandi. The light over the third camera blinked on.

"My other guest this morning doesn't view *A Dream of Darkness* from quite the same perspective as Damion Tanner does. In fact, she has some very specific objections to Mr. Tanner's role in that movie. Welcome to our program, Sandi."

"Thank you."

Mark gestured toward her. "Dr. Alessandra Hawkins works at the Laurence Clinic here in Los Angeles. She is a psychologist with a doctoral degree in family counseling. Her doctoral dissertation dealt with the classification of psychogenic female sexual dysfunction." Mark's smile became wolfish. "In layman's terms we would call her a sex therapist."

Sandi heard a brief, strangled gasp from Damion's direction. Mark Kline ignored the sound as he leaned toward her.

"Dr. Hawkins, would you explain to us why you find *A Dream of Darkness* such a disturbing movie?"

At that moment Sandi would willingly have handed over her life savings to get herself off the show. She wished fervently that she were a hundred miles away from the studio and a million miles away from Damion Tanner. Fervent wishes, however, were not going to change the situation she had gotten herself into. She drew in a deep breath, determined to speak clearly and professionally. She wasn't going to blow her chance to convey an important message to the millions of people watching Mark Kline's program.

"There are many aspects of *A Dream of Darkness* that

I admire," she said, "but I think it provides a potentially harmful view of human sexual relations. In my work at the Laurence Clinic I encounter more and more young people who have what we therapists call performance anxiety. These young people are afraid to commit themselves to an intimate relationship because they know they won't be able to live up to the unrealistic expectations raised by movies like *A Dream of Darkness*. More specifically, they know they can never achieve the standards of apparent sensuality set by actors like Mr. Tanner."

"*Apparent* sensuality?" Mark Kline murmured.

"There is no evidence that in real-life situations Mr. Tanner's sexual expertise lives up to the standard portrayed so graphically in the movie."

Damion leaned forward in his chair. "Were you hoping for a real-life demonstration?" he drawled.

Sandi was furious at the blush she could feel rising in her cheeks. "No, Mr. Tanner, I was not."

"Just checking, honey. I never like to turn down a lady."

The audience tittered, and Sandi thought murderous thoughts. If he called her *honey* one more time, she wouldn't be answerable for the consequences.

Mark Kline's intervention saved her from saying something she would certainly have regretted. "Would you tell us precisely why you find Mr. Tanner's performance so unsettling, Dr. Hawkins?"

"Certainly. There is a myth circulating in America that the sexual revolution of the seventies solved all our sexual problems and set everybody free to pursue happiness. In fact, psychologists like me who work with troubled individuals and disturbed families have found that relations between the sexes are not necessarily improving."

"Why do you think this is, Dr. Hawkins?"

"I think the media have a lot to answer for. It's no secret that sex is used to sell everything from cheese-flavored crackers to political candidates. Television, Hollywood, and the advertising agencies all convey the not-so-subtle message that people have an obligation to make the most of themselves. That probably wouldn't be all bad, except that the media emphasize our bodies at the expense of our minds and our hearts. We're never told that we have to be kind or thoughtful toward others. We're rarely told that we ought to be better informed or educated. But we're told daily, in a hundred different ways, that we have a duty to be beautiful, athletic, thin, pimple-free, deodorized, and glamorous. Above all, we're told that we have an obligation to be sexy."

"Is that such a bad message?" Mark Kline asked. "After all, there's no particular harm in encouraging people to make themselves as attractive as possible."

"In a limited sort of way I probably agree with you. And of course many people are confident enough to ignore the message when it becomes a bit too heavy for them. But for the patients who end up in the Laurence Clinic, and for many others who don't seek treatment, the message leads to disaster. Movies like *A Dream of Darkness* tell young men that in order to be successful human beings, they must look as attractive and as seductive as Mr. Tanner. Unfortunately for most people that's an impossible goal. No matter how many hours they spend in the gym, no matter how much revitalizing shampoo they use, they are never going to look like Damion Tanner. Their genes are against them."

Damion bared his teeth. "I'm thrilled to know that you find me so irresistible, Dr. Hawkins."

She bared her teeth in return. "I don't find you irresistible, Mr. Tanner. I said that young people, who don't know any better, wish they could look like you."

"According to you, these hordes of misguided young people don't just want to look like me. They wish they could make love like me, too."

"You misunderstood my remarks, Mr. Tanner. I'm

sure you make love just like anybody else, maybe even less effectively than most of my clients. But many young people don't realize that. They watch you seduce a woman in the movie, and they forget that you played the scene with the benefit of ten people directing your actions to ensure the maximum erotic effect. They forget that there's mood music swelling to a crescendo at just the right moment. They forget that the electrician worked for five hours adjusting the lighting on the set until it created the perfect luminous glow. They forget that the cameraman adjusted his focus and his filters, and the makeup artist spent half the day working over your body to get just the right sheen on your skin."

"Hey, honey," Damion said softly, "How many times did you have to watch me make love before you got that list down so pat?"

"My name," she hissed, "is not honey. For your information, Mr. Tanner, it is *Doctor* Alessandra Hawkins."

Damion leaned across Mark Kline's chair. His eyes wrapped her in an intimacy that denied the existence of the studio audience and several million television viewers. "*Doctor* Alessandra Hawkins," he repeated softly, "how many times did you have to watch me make love before you got that list down so pat?"

There was genuine regret in Mark Kline's voice when he stretched out his hand, gesturing Sandi to remain silent. "Ladies and gentlemen, I'm afraid I have to call a halt to our discussion right at this fascinating point. Dr. Hawkins, Damion Tanner, I'm grateful to you for your time and for your insights."

Sandi closed her ears to the remainder of his patter. She was angry, and she didn't know whether to direct her anger at herself, at Damion, or even at Mark Kline, who had engineered their confrontation. The producer signaled another commercial break, and an assistant arrived to escort her and Damion from the set.

"Would you like some coffee or a sweet roll?" the assistant asked as soon as they reached the lounge.

"Thank you, but I have to get back to work," Sandi said. She was anxious to put the maximum possible distance between herself and Damion Tanner. "Good-bye, Damion."

Walking out of the lounge without once looking back, she was startled when she reached the elevator and found Damion standing right beside her. She punched the call button with a great deal more force than was necessary.

"Half the gossip columnists in the United States watch that show," he said abruptly. "Do you realize what you've just done?"

"Movies thrive on publicity," she said, sounding calmer than she felt. "It doesn't matter whether it's good publicity or bad."

The elevator arrived, and they both stepped inside. "It matters to me," he said tersely. "You know as well as I do how the gossip columnists operate. It will take them approximately two and a half seconds to discover that you're Richard Hawkins's daughter. Then it will take about three more seconds before the presses roll into action: 'Director's daughter accuses movie star of being oversexed and underendowed.' That's probably the least suggestive of the headlines they'll come up with."

She swallowed hard. "As long as the box office cash registers keep ringing, why should you care?"

"Leaving my feelings aside, have you forgotten that it's your father's script that you were tearing to pieces back there? He was trying to tell a serious story, and he won an Oscar for his efforts. But thanks to you, by the time the supermarket tabloids have finished embroidering your comments, half the public will be wondering if this year's Academy Award went to a porno star."

The elevator stopped, and Sandi stalked out. *"A Dream of Darkness* is an interesting movie," she said, "but I don't think it needed quite so many close-ups of you touching Julie Blake and Julie collapsing into instant ecstasy. I don't suppose you're interested in scientific facts, but for your information, woman are physically incapable of that sort of instantaneous response."

"The more I listen to you, *Doctor* Hawkins, the more convinced I am that you're suffering from a bad case of sexual repression. The movie wasn't intended as an illustrated manual for a sex education class; it was intended as entertainment. As far as I can see, you're mighty hung up on something that was only a detail in the main thrust of the plot. What's your problem, Doctor? Are you one of those people who takes out her frustrations by criticizing other people's sexual activities?"

Sandi marched across the parking lot, shaking with fury. "No, I'm not," she said. "But even if I were, I'd still be a whole heap better off than you are. At least I don't have to hide my fears of sexual inadequacy behind a series of fake come-ons."

His voice became dangerously quiet. "What, *precisely,* are you suggesting, Dr. Hawkins?"

She shrugged. "I've been doing some research recently, and I've come to the conclusion that some of Hollywood's most publicized sex symbols have very unsatisfactory real-life relationships. They switch partners so frequently because they're always hoping to find somebody who'll provide the magic that they're unable to provide for themselves."

"Is that a polite way of suggesting that I'm sexually inadequate, Dr. Hawkins?"

Her green eyes clashed with his. "You said it, Mr. Tanner, not me."

His expression hardened into one of contempt. "Just for the record, Doctor, I would like to state categorically that my performance in front of the cameras doesn't hide any fear of sexual inadequacy. In fact, I'm confident that I could seduce any unattached woman I set my mind to seducing. And, contrary to your supposition, I could do it without the benefit of makeup artists, fancy lighting, or even a director to tell me where to put my hands."

She leaned against the door of her car, feigning a casualness she was light-years away from feeling. "That's an easy claim to make when you know very well that I have no way of putting it to the test."

There was a slight pause. "Oh, but you do," he said finally. "You're an unattached female, Dr. Hawkins, and I assume your biological functions are normal."

"What has that got to do with anything?"

"It's got everything to do with the subject we're discussing. I'm making you a proposition, Dr. Hawkins. I'll try my best to seduce you. You try your best to resist me. We should soon see whose performance statistics hold up better."

She jabbed her key into the car door so viciously that she scratched the paint around the lock. It was the only mark on the entire surface of the car, and it suddenly seemed inevitable to her that Damion should have caused it.

"That's an absolutely ridiculous suggestion!" she exclaimed furiously. "And for heaven's sake stoping calling me *Doctor* Hawkins!"

"I could have sworn that *Doctor* Hawkins was what you ordered me to call you."

"That was on a TV show, for goodness' sake! My name's Sandi. Is that such a difficult name to remember?"

"Not at all. In fact, it's amazingly easy." He laughed softly. "Well, do we have a deal, Sandi?"

"No, of course we don't. Now, if you'll excuse me, Damion, I'm already late, and I have clients waiting who really need my time. I've already wasted too much of this morning."

He didn't answer at once. Instead he reached out and crooked his forefinger beneath her chin, gently pulling her face around and studying it for a long time. "Frightened, Sandi?" he murmured at last.

"Of course not."

"Then why not agree to the experiment? Think what an interesting footnote it would make to your research project."

She knew she needed to answer him quickly, before the touch of his finger against her skin caused permanent brain damage. Thank God she had enough common sense left to say no to his ridiculous proposition.

"All right, Damion," she said huskily. "You have a deal."

She heard herself speak the words, but she couldn't quite believe she'd said them. Flustered, she eased her chin away from his caressing finger, and coherent thought immediately became easier.

"You'll regret your challenge, Damion, but I promise to disguise your identity when I make my report, so nobody will know but me."

"That's very considerate of you," he murmured. "But unnecessary, since I don't plan to regret anything."

There was no longer any point of physical contact between them, but the warmth of his body seemed to radiate outward, leaping over the gap that separated them like heat searing a path in front of a forest fire. Her mind warned her that it was time to flee, but her body seemed to have no interest in cooperating. She sensed the danger approaching, but she couldn't escape it. Worse, she didn't want to escape it. She discovered to her horror that she actually wanted to get burned.

She closed her eyes for an instant, and when she opened them again the look in his eyes made her wish she'd been smart enough to run when she still had the chance. Slowly he clasped his hands around her waist, and his head descended until his lips hovered no more than a breath away from hers. He brushed his lips across her mouth with tantalizing, exasperating lightness. Aching, throbbing, she waited for him to deepen the kiss.

He raised his head. "Good-bye, Sandi," he said

roughly. "I'll give you a call some time this evening to set up our first date."

"No . . . wait! Damion, I can't . . . I haven't agreed . . ."

His hands fell back to his sides, but the imprint of his touch was etched deep into her body.

"Until tonight, Sandi," he said, and strode quickly across the parking lot before she could retract her rash promise.

Chapter Five

SANDI HAD NO sooner set her car in motion than she realized just how much she regretted having accepted Damion's absurd challenge. She couldn't understand how she had agreed to do something so totally out of character. Her work as a sex therapist was provocative by nature, and the results of her research were often open to misinterpretation. Because of that, she had always been especially careful not to compromise the dignity of her patients or the clinical detachment with which she handled her research projects. Acute temporary insanity seemed the only explanation for her agreement to Damion's crazy proposition.

She parked her car in the shade of an oleander bush and walked briskly into the clinic, her common sense gradually returning. There was really no point in getting hot and bothered over something essentially trivial, she decided. Damion Tanner would never call her, so why waste any more time thinking about their ridiculous bet?

She greeted her secretary with a courteous smile and flipped open her engagement calendar as she scanned the pile of incoming mail. Her schedule today, like most days, was certain to be hectic. Her first appointment was with a young couple whose marriage remained unconsummated six months after the wedding ceremony. In a world where the media reported at length on twelve-year-olds seeking abortions and TV personalities contemplating their fourth or fifth marriages, Sandi had discovered that a surprising number of people were still so inhibited, or so plain ignorant about the functioning of their bodies, that they could not enjoy a normal sexual relationship.

Her first clients would arrive in a couple of minutes, but the image of Damion's mocking smile thrust itself into her consciousness with infuriating persistence. Damn the man! What could she have been thinking of when she agreed to his absurd bet?

She pressed the buzzer on her desk, letting the receptionist know she was ready to see her clients. There was no reason in the world to think about Damion. If he actually called, she wouldn't accept his invitation. Fatigue-induced insanity could only last so long.

Coming from a family like hers, Sandi thought wryly, she certainly needed to remain sane. She remembered that her mother still hadn't agreed to the gallstone operation, and her mind spiraled off into a new set of worries. She reflected ruefully that worrying about her mother made a pleasant change from worrying about her crazy reactions to Damion Tanner. It was a bit like the Chinese cure for a headache: drop something heavy on your toe, so you'll have a different pain to think about.

The phone rang at midnight, an hour and a half after Sandi had gone to bed. She grabbed the receiver, fearing an emergency call from Italy, but it wasn't her mother or a doctor; it was Damion. She recognized his deep voice instantly, and her stomach gave an infuriating leap of excitement. Leaning back against the pillows, she unthinkingly closed her eyes and cradled the receiver against her cheek.

"Hello, Sandi," he murmured. "It's late to call, but I've been out all evening and I didn't want you to fall asleep without knowing that I was thinking about you. I missed you today. I hope you've missed me, too."

She moistened her suddenly dry lips. "I . . . thought about you," she admitted.

"I'm glad," he said huskily. "Do you know what I've been doing for the past fifteen minutes? I've been lying here in my lonely bed, imagining how you would feel curled up beside me. I imagined your hair spread out on the pillow and the swell of your breasts cupped in my hands. I imagined what it would be like to kiss you, to feel your lips parting beneath mine as your body started to tremble with passion. I want you, Sandi. I can't sleep because I want to make love to you so badly."

The rough vibrations of his voice found an echo in every hidden recess of her body, and she sighed tremulously. Fortunately the mists of sleep cleared from her brain just in time to prevent disaster. She sat bolt upright in the bed, rubbing her eyes fiercely. Good grief, what was happening to her? How could she have forgotten their bet? She couldn't possibly be falling for such a corny routine! His patter sounded like the worst scene in a badly written soap opera.

She thought rapidly. "Why, Peter," she cooed softly, "how nice of you to call! I've been thinking about you all day long, wondering where you were. We always have such fantastic times together." She allowed her voice to drift into a sensuous, throaty murmur. "Of course I miss you, Peter. How could you ask? When did you get back in town?"

There was a brief moment of silence on the other end of the line, followed by the distinct sound of rustling bedcovers. Sandi smiled tightly. Good! At least she'd managed to make the arrogant devil sit up.

The rustling stopped. "This isn't Peter," he said curtly. "This is Damion."

"Damion? Damion Tanner?" She managed to inject just the right note of drowsy bewilderment into her question. "Good heavens, Damion, I was asleep! Why on earth are you calling me at this hour?"

"I'm not sure anymore." To her surprise, he sounded amused rather than offended. "It seemed like a good idea when I dialed the number. I'm sorry I woke you. Who's Peter?"

"Peter? Oh, he's just a good friend," she said airily. "A *good* friend. He—um—travels a lot, so I never know when he's going to be in town."

"I see. Well, since Peter isn't here, will you have dinner with me tomorrow night? I know a great place run by a Vietnamese immigrant who specializes in French cooking with an Oriental flair. I think you'd like it."

Sandi reminded herself that his invitation was simply the first move in his planned campaign of seduction. She reminded herself that she had a long, proud record of behaving rationally despite numerous temptations to act otherwise. She was fairly confident that if she said no to this suggestion, Damion would never call her back. She twisted the telephone cord around her fingers, trying to convince herself that this wasn't the moment to break a twenty-eight year habit of making practical, sensible decisions. She thought about her father's six wives and her mother's innumerable lovers, and her resolution hardened. She spoke quickly, refusing to acknowledge a tiny, irrational feeling of regret.

"Thanks for the invitation, Damion, but I don't think it would be a good idea for us to go out together. We really have nothing in common."

"Reneging on our bet?" he asked softly. "Are you so scared of what might happen that you're willing to concede victory before the first battle?"

"I'm not scared of anything," she said tartly. "This isn't a military campaign, Damion. It isn't even a question of winning and losing. It's a question of how we organize our lives. We both acted foolishly this morning. I realize that now."

"Yes, I rather think we did."

"There you are, then," she said, wondering why his prompt agreement so depressed her. "Look, Damion, you're a Hollywood golden boy, with the world at your fingertips. Any starlet in California would faint with happiness if you asked her out, so I'm sure you have better ways to spend your time than in attempting to seduce me. And I certainly have better things to do than waste a whole evening resisting you just to prove some academic point."

"I agree," he murmured. "So don't bother to resist, honey, and we'll both have a fabulous night. I guarantee it."

Irritation at his colossal arrogance replaced all her other tangled emotions. "You know, Damion, if you really believe you can guarantee my pleasure—or any woman's pleasure, for that matter—I almost feel sorry for you. With all the experience you've had, haven't you realized yet that it takes two caring and committed people to make love? Even a brief sexual encounter requires consideration and thoughtfulness from both partners if it's to be satisfactory. For your information, one self-satisfied stud with a muscled body and an inflated ego won't do the trick. Sexual athletics on the part of the man, however talented he might be, will never ensure pleasure for the woman. So I'm afraid your guarantee is an empty one, Damion."

"Then show me how to give you pleasure, Sandi. Teach me how to make love the way you like it, the way you think it ought to be."

Her fingers closed tightly around the phone, and she swallowed hard. His voice, she thought despairingly, ought to be licensed as a lethal weapon. "If you're asking for professional counseling, Mr. Tanner, my fee is a hundred and fifty dollars an hour, plus expenses. I'm assuming, of course, that you aren't eligble for the discounts we give to clients who can't afford my regular fee."

"I don't suppose I'm eligible for any discounts, but I'm sure your advice is a bargain, whatever the price. I'll pick you up tomorrow at seven-thirty at your apartment, and we'll discuss scheduling over dinner. I'm looking forward to my first lesson. Good night, Sandi."

He hung up before she had time to refuse. Or, as she admitted to herself later, he hung up while she remained silent on her end of the line. Which, when she thought about it, was an uncomfortable distinction.

In Sandi's experience, movie stars always arrived late in order to impress people with their importance. She calculated that Damion, as the winner of this year's Oscar, would turn up at least forty-five minutes behind schedule, carrying an armful of expensive flowers and eager to shower her with elaborate, insincere apologies.

In actuality he surprised her by arriving two minutes early and bringing no gift of any sort. His clothing, however, fit every one of her worst preconceptions. He wore skintight black jeans with a custom label sewn on the front as well as on the back pocket, and a black velour turtleneck with two golden zippers slashed diagonally from shoulder to waist. One zipper was partly undone, revealing a tantalizing glimpse of tanned masculine chest. He carried short black leather driving gloves, and his hair had been blow-dried into a casual, windswept look that must have taken at least an hour to produce. Despite the fact that it was already evening, his eyes were hidden behind huge aviator sunglasses.

Somehow she knew instinctively that he had chosen his outfit expressly to annoy her, and her mouth curved into a tiny, reluctant smile. "Trying out for a part as a cat burglar?" she asked as he strolled into her living room.

He took off his sunglasses and allowed his gaze to roam slowly over her. His mocking blue eyes rested first on the tight, immaculate twist of her hair, then moved to her plain gray silk dress and matching shoes. He finally looked at her face.

"No," he said with perfect gravity. "Are you trying out for a part as a nun?"

She laughed out loud, unable to help herself. "All right, Damion, you win this round. But could you please leave your sunglasses in the car while we eat dinner?"

The intensity of his gaze suddenly made her knees shake. "Certainly I'll leave them," he said. "Tonight I want only to please you."

Sensing a double meaning in his words, she turned away with the excuse of picking up her woolen evening jacket. Heat rippled under her skin, carrying prickles of desire. The trouble was, she thought wryly, when she was near Damion, she would probably suspect a sexy double meaning if he started to recite the alphabet.

When they arrived at the restaurant, the head waiter greeted them with great deference and immediately seated them in a quiet, secluded corner booth. The place was crowded with elegant diners, but Damion made absolutely no effort to draw attention to himself, which Sandi found a refreshing change from many of the actors she knew.

The owner himself came out to hand them their menus. "Mr. Tanner," he said, "we congratulate you on your great success at the Oscar ceremony. My daughter wishes me to thank you for the autographed picture you sent her. She is the envy of all her friends."

"It's my pleasure," Damion said easily. "How are you doing, Ben? It looks as if business is booming."

"It has been excellent since you were kind enough to start recommending us to your friends. Last Saturday I was forced to turn away at least half a dozen bookings, including a request by Farrah Fawcett's hairdresser. Six months ago I could not have dreamed of such prosperity."

Damion grinned. "When Hollywood hairdressers start calling, you know you've reached the pinnacle of success! I'll have to stop recommending your cooking before this place gets too popular. I'll soon have to call a month in advance to get a reservation."

"For you, Mr. Tanner, there is always a table." Ben bowed as he was summoned away by an urgent message from the kitchen, and Sandi picked up the thick leather-bound menu.

"Your friend speaks excellent English," she remarked.

"Ben went to college in the States back in the late fifties, so when he arrived here after the fall of Saigon, he had a head start over most of his fellow refugees. In the last eight years he's put three of his children and two of his sisters through college. He also happens to be one of the best chefs in California. I think you'll agree after you've tasted his food."

They selected a first course of shrimp lightly flavored with ginger and a main course of baked veal stuffed with spinach and ground almonds. When they had ordered, Damion leaned forward and circled his thumb gently over Sandi's knuckles. Striving for the appearance of calm, she removed her hand and picked up her glass, swallowing several quick mouthfuls of ice water. Damion's superabundant supply of pheromones didn't seem to have diminished in the slightest since yesterday morning. She reflected ruefully that at least moths and toads had the consideration to produce their sexual hormones on a cyclical basis.

Damion ordered a bottle of white wine without making a huge production of it, then leaned back against the velvet-upholstered seat. "So tell me something about yourself, Sandi. How did you end up as a sex therapist? Were you always interested in psychology?"

"Not at all. In fact, math was my best subject in high

school, and I started out as a science major at UCLA. I had some vague hope of becoming an astrophysicist and discovering something startling about the origin of the universe. If not another Einstein, I was going to be at least a rival to Carl Sagan."

"I guess the stars seemed pleasantly remote and predictable in comparison to human beings. Living with Richard Hawkins and Gabriella Barini can't have been easy."

"Perhaps not." She looked up, somewhat startled by his perception. Even people who had known her for years never realized just why she had found the immutable order of the heavens so appealing. They had never seen the connection between her father's third marriage to an explosive young rock singer and Sandi's pleasure in the logic and security of scientific equations.

"What caused you to switch to psychology?" Damion asked. "Did people suddenly seem more interesting than planets after all?"

"I don't think so. I guess the reasons for the switch were pretty much what you could expect from an eighteen-year-old college student."

"The psychology professor was younger and cuter than the physics professor?"

She smiled. "Even less worthy than that. About halfway through my second year it dawned on me that I stayed up all night studying and barely scraped through with C's in physics, whereas I made straight A's in all the psychology courses without even reading the textbooks! At the end of the semester I changed my major, and eventually went on to earn a graduate degree in psychology. It wasn't until I started the graduate program that I realized just how much I enjoyed working with people and helping them think through their problems. Almost before I realized what was happening, I had my doctorate and a state license to work as a counselor."

She paused when the waiter brought them their shrimp,

but Damion returned to the subject of her career as soon as they were alone again.

"Surely something specific must have made you decide to become a sex therapist. That doesn't seem the sort of career you drift into just because you happen to be making good grades in psychology."

She hesitated, then shrugged slightly as she produced her standard response. She had already revealed far more than she had intended. "My job title at the clinic makes my work sound more specialized than it really is, Damion. Most psychologists who work with adults spend quite a lot of their time advising their clients on sexual matters. I'm basically a family counselor as much as I'm anything else."

"It sure didn't sound that way when Mark Kline was describing your expertise on his television show."

"Damion, for heaven's sake! You of all people ought to know how easily facts get distorted on a talk show."

Grateful when they were interrupted by the arrival of their main course, she deliberately switched the conversation to Damion's career. After years of listening to her parents and their friends, she knew that few actors could resist talking about their triumphs.

Damion, she soon discovered, was somewhat of an exception. He was willing enough to talk, but she could sense the twin threads of self-mockery and reserve that ran through his speech. His conversation was amusing, but she found herself wishing he would let down his facade and allow her to see the real man who hid behind the cool, sardonic mask.

"What happened after your outstanding success as the Halloween witch?" she asked, once they had sampled the excellent veal. "Was there a talent scout in the audience who whisked you straight off to fame and fortune in New York?"

Damion grinned. "If there'd been a talent scout in the audience, I'm sure he'd have been smart enough not to offer me a contract. Let me remind you that I was chosen to play the witch because I was tall, not because I could act."

She laughed. "Well, after your brief moment of glory, what did you do next? Did they need a tall Wise Man for the Christmas pageant?"

He spent an inordinate amount of time studying a broiled mushroom. "I got married," he said finally. "We were divorced three years later."

"I'm sorry," she said quietly. "I didn't know you were married, Damion."

He shrugged with apparent indifference. "It happened a long time ago," he said lightly. "Even the scandal sheets have found it hard to dig up anything interesting to report about my marriage. There was no reason for you to know about it."

"How old were you when you married? Nineteen? Did you have to drop out of school?"

"No. My parents were delighted to continue supporting us, and I was immature enough to accept their money without thinking much about it. Janet and I stayed on in Cleveland. She was an elementary education major, and I was spending almost all my time with the university drama club. At the end of my second year our school joined with a couple of other local colleges to put on a full-scale production of *Macbeth*."

"That was pretty ambitious, wasn't it?"

"It was more than ambitious; it was ridiculous. But we were basically too ignorant to understand what we'd undertaken. Do you remember Art Berenstein? He'd once been a famous New York director, and he happened to be the artist-in-residence at the university. He undertook to produce the entire show. He was at least eighty years old, and he'd been retired for the best part of ten years. On his good days he was sober until midafternoon; on his bad days he was drunk before lunch time. He called about a dozen young hopefuls to audition for the lead, but he never asked a single one of us to read anything from the play. He'd decided he wanted Macbeth to be tall with black hair and blue eyes. As soon as he saw me, he announced I had the part."

"Weren't you pleased?"

"On the contrary, I was deeply insulted. I'd spent three weeks rehearsing Macbeth's big speech, and here I was, hired because of the color of my eyes. I demanded that he listen to me recite."

"What happened?"

"He refused point blank. He said that since there wasn't the slightest possibility that any student would be capable of acting the part of Macbeth, it didn't matter who messed up the role. He added that at least I looked vaguely Gaelic, which meant that I would give a better showing than any of the other students who'd turned up for the audition. 'You've got good legs, boy,' he said. 'You can wear tights. Your calf muscles are solid.'"

She laughed. "I can't guess the end of this story. Was the show a monumental failure or a great triumph?"

"Oh, it was a triumph, of course. How could it have been anything else with my Gaelic calf muscles *and* Art Berenstein's direction? When Art was sober, he was incandescent. Even when he was drunk, he came pretty close to brilliance. Of course, I didn't see it that way at the time. I just thought of him as a crabby old man who was forever putting me down. My pride was wounded, you see, because he wasn't at all impressed with my acting ability. He didn't seem to care that I was considered the best actor on campus. I was determined to prove to that doddery old has-been just what a brilliant actor I was, so I worked my butt off, practicing the role night and day. I spent hours and hours in front of the mirror, perfecting my gestures. More hours in the rehearsal room projecting my voice until I could be heard at the back of the gallery without shouting. More hours brooding over my copy of the play, trying to discover every nuance of

Shakespeare's meaning. In the end the student newspapers were rhapsodic about the entire production, and the most prestigious local drama critic announced that 'Mr. Tanner gave the most mature and sensitive interpretation of this difficult role that I have ever seen in a college production.'"

"I hope Art Berenstein was suitably impressed?"

"I wouldn't say *impressed* is quite the right word. I took the pile of reviews to him and waved them triumphantly under his nose." Damion's eyes gleamed with silent laughter. "He pushed them to one side and said, 'Young man, despite what these amateur critics have to say, right now you have just about enough real acting talent to play a horse's arse. The front end would be too difficult for you. In thirty years' time, if you work damned hard, maybe you'll be fit to play Macbeth, but I doubt it.'"

"Despite everything, I have the feeling you admired him enormously."

"You're right, I did. Even at the time, in some hidden corner of my mind, I recognized that he was paying me a great compliment by telling me the truth about my so-called talent. Of course I wasn't capable of playing Macbeth at that stage in my career, although I think maybe I was just about ready to play the head and shoulders of a horse."

"I seem to remember reading Art Berenstein's obituary quite a while back."

"Yes, he died five years ago, clutching a whiskey bottle. I still miss him. Despite all his harsh comments, he was the one who got me my first New York role. It was Off-Off-Broadway, but I did get paid, so after that I could claim professional experience."

"I'm almost afraid to ask what role he found you."

"Not the rear end of a horse, although it came pretty close. It was a typical Off-Off-Broadway production, full of deep hidden meaning and long, boring speeches. I played a garbage collector whose best friend was a pet rat he'd rescued from a garbage can."

"Something tells me the play didn't run long."

"Three weeks, which is a fairly decent run for an Off-Off-Broadway show. And the reviews were amazingly favorable, which has made me suspicious of critics ever since."

"It would have been great if Art could have seen you win the Oscar."

"Are you kidding? He'd probably have said something so shattering that my ego would never have recovered."

Sandi laughed. "I don't think your ego is so easily shattered." She took a sip of the espresso the waiter had brought. "What did your wife think of your first role on the professional stage? I'm guessing she liked you as Macbeth better."

"Janet never came to New York," Damion said briefly. He drained his cup of coffee, then turned away to summon the waiter. "If you don't want dessert, Sandi, shall we collect the check and go home? I have an early start tomorrow morning and I'm sure you do, too."

"Er . . . yes. Yes, I'd certainly like to get home at a reasonable hour."

They settled silently into his car, a black Porsche with a scarlet interior. Sandi wanted to make some joking comment about the blatant sensuality of the red plush seats and the black suede roof, but her teasing words died away unspoken. She was uncomfortably tense, more ill at ease than she cared to admit. Damion's clothes and his car fit the stereotype that she wanted to put him in, a stereotype that she found extremely easy to resist. But so far the evening had not followed her expectations in almost any other regard. Far from trying to seduce her by staring into her eyes and whispering sweet nothings, Damion had directed a conversation that had been about as far removed from the romantic as it was possible to imagine. It was as if he had reached out and tried to touch her mind rather than her body. The truth was that she had found their time together fascinating.

Sandi stirred restlessly in the low-slung seat, then turned to stare at the cars rushing by on the dark, neon-lit freeway. It was much safer to look at the cars than at Damion's perfect profile. Fascination, as she regularly told her patients and her students, was an inappropriate basis for any adult relationship, since proximity soon caused the fascination to wear off, usually leaving boredom and disillusion in its wake.

The silence of their journey home was just what she needed to get her feelings back into proper perspective, Sandi concluded, and she was fully in control of herself when Damion drew the Porsche to a halt outside her apartment building. She pulled her woolen cape tightly around her shoulders and tucked her evening purse under her arm as soon as Damion turned off the ignition.

"Thank you for going out with me this evening," he said softly. "I enjoyed our time together very much."

"I enjoyed myself, too." She edged toward the door, waiting for him to make his move. But he didn't try to take her into his arms, nor did he invite himself up to her apartment. The silence stretched out uncomfortably, and she pushed a stray lock of hair back behind her ear.

"Well, as you mentioned, Damion, we both have early appointments . . ."

His blue eyes were unfathomable as his gaze skimmed over her, and heat flared disturbingly beneath her skin.

"Why do you keep moving away from me?" he asked quietly.

"I wasn't aware I was doing that," she said, trying to sound cool and self-possessed. "Anyway, thank you again for a lovely evening."

His hand closed tightly on the steering wheel. "Please don't mouth platitudes at me, Sandi. I don't think either of us wants to admit what we're feeling, but that's no reason to take refuge in meaningless pleasantries. We owe each other a little more honesty than that."

She drew in a quick, sharp breath. "We owe each other nothing, Damion, except thanks for an enjoyable evening."

"If that's true, then why are you so nervous?"

She swallowed hard. "Because of that ridiculous bet," she admitted. "I don't know why we made it."

"Our behavior yesterday was certainly a bit irrational," he agreed. "But then, strong emotions tend to give rise to irrational behavior, wouldn't you agree?"

"If we have any special feelings for each other, Damion, I think we both know they're negative ones."

He didn't deny her assertion. "Instant mutual dislike can be as potent a force as instant attraction," he said quietly. "You're the psychologist, Dr. Hawkins. Explain to me what reasons we might have for disliking each other."

"There could be a thousand different explanations," she said crisply, with feigned self-possession. "Perhaps you distrust all psychologists. Perhaps I remind you of a kindergarten teacher you disliked. Or perhaps you subconsciously remind me of the high school jock who always pulled my ponytail."

"Maybe," he said huskily. "Or maybe we resent the intensity of the emotions we arouse in each other. Didn't your professors ever teach you that we don't always like the people we desire, Dr. Hawkins?"

"Yes," she said. "But we're human beings, not animals, and my professors also taught me that we should never become physically involved with people we don't like."

"Physically involved," he murmured. "Now there's a nice, dry, clinical term. But I don't think it really describes how you and I feel toward each other." In the darkness of the car, the brilliance of his eyes seemed to become more shadowed, and the tautness of his features blurred into momentary softness. "For once in your life,

Doctor, why don't you stop analyzing your emotions and just let yourself feel?"

Some new and indefinable tension entered the air between them. He touched his fingertips to her throat, stroking her skin softly until a dozen different pulses began to quiver in unison with the movement of his hands. In a minute, she thought, in less than a minute, she would definitely get out of the car. She would tell him right now that she was leaving. It was ridiculous for her to stay.

"Dr. Hawkins," he whispered, his breath warm against her cheek, "shall I tell you what we both felt for each other the first time we met?"

"No," she croaked, forcing her few functioning brain cells into action. "No, I don't want to talk about it."

"Perhaps you'd prefer that I show you what we both wanted? What we both still want?"

"No..."

"Sandi, my sweet, I'll have to give you lessons on how to say yes. It's quite easy once you get the hang of it." Laughter danced in his eyes as he cupped her face between his hands. His thumbs traced a series of erotic circles on her cheeks before moving to the corners of her mouth.

"You have to place your lips just so," he murmured, pressing gently. "Now breathe deeply and try to say the magic word."

Her remaining brain cells slowly dissolved into little centers of enchantment, depriving her of all power of speech, even the vital power to say no. She closed her eyes, and her head tilted involuntarily backward, baring her throat to his caressing fingers. If only he would keep his fingers still, she was quite sure she could speak, but the seductive movement of his hands never stopped. He continued to stroke her even when he moved suddenly to take the pins from her hair. She shivered with a sweet wave of pleasure as he loosened her chignon and gently pulled the long, dark brown strands over her shoulders.

"You have beautiful hair," he said huskily. "When I imagined it spread out over my pillow, I didn't begin to do justice to the reality."

Though still unable to speak, she managed finally to open her eyes. The move was not necessarily a wise one. Even in the dim light filtering into the car, she could see the slashes of passionate color that darkened his high cheekbones, and her pulse began to race in instinctive response. She reached out, hesitantly tracing the faint lines that radiated from his eyes. It was intoxicating to feel him shudder at her light touch.

"Open your mouth," he whispered thickly. "I want to kiss you."

His hands slid downward to cup her breasts, and his thumbs moved over her nipples in an expert, knowing caress. There was no way to conceal her immediate physical reaction.

"Tell me this is what you wanted, Sandi," he murmured. "Tell me this is what you've needed from the moment we first met. Let me come up to your apartment. I promise we'll do only what you want; we'll make love in the ways that please you most."

His practiced, seductive words dropped like stones into the sudden stillness of her mind, and her body froze into total, icy rejection. The very expertise of his touch reminded her, just in time, that Damion wasn't making love to *her*, he was merely seducing her body in pursuit of a bet that threatened his masculine ego. Horrified at what she had allowed to happen, she pulled herself out of his arms and pressed against the car door as she fumbled to restore some sort of order to her flowing hair. To her chagrin, even through her intense anger, she was aware that her body cried out in frustration at the loss of Damion's touch.

She clutched her evening cape so tightly that her fingers felt numb. "That was an excellent try, Damion," she said coolly, "but you forgot something crucial. I'm trained to recognize the techniques of seduction, even when they're applied as expertly as you apply them."

For a split second he remained absolutely still. Then he passed his hand over his eyes, concealing them for an instant before he turned away. Finally he turned around, running his hand through his hair with a careless gesture. "I guess I should be flattered," he drawled. "Not every student gets such good grades on his first attempt. What do you recommend I work on next, if I want to improve?"

"How about a touch of genuine emotion to back up the technical expertise?" she said coldly.

His blue gaze was brilliant with mockery. "Sandi, honey, you should know better than to make such a foolish suggestion. Genuine emotion is forbidden by union rules, and probably outlawed under the state. constitution. You could get me drummed out of Hollywood if I accepted advice like that."

Sandi realized suddenly that she felt sick. She bent to pick up her purse and with a quick shrug of his shoulders, Damion got out of the car, walking around courteously to open the door for her.

They didn't speak as he escorted her into the building lobby. The doorman, who had probably observed their prolonged farewell with considerable interest, Sandi decided, looked discreetly away. His tact was unnecessary. Damion placed his hands lightly on her shoulders and dropped a brief, impersonal kiss on her cheek.

"Thanks again for an enjoyable evening," he said. "I'll be in touch."

"Of course," Sandi said dryly. "Good-bye, Damion." The steadiness of her voice belied her tumultuous feelings, and she walked purposefully to the elevators without once looking back.

She unlocked her apartment door, congratulating herself on having successfully resisted seduction by Damion Tanner, Hollywood's latest gift to the fantasy life of

American women. It was another wise decision in a lifetime dedicated to making wise, sensible decisions.

And if she worked on it for the next dozen years or so, she might even convince herself that she was thrilled to be spending the night alone.

Chapter Six

SINCE HER RETURN from Italy, Sandi had made five phone calls and paid two visits to her father's house without ever finding him available. She finally managed to catch him alone in his office the day after her date with Damion.

"Why, hello, kid," he said as his secretary showed her in. "I wasn't expecting to see you today. Linda's joining me for lunch at Rinaldo's. Would you like to come with us?"

"No, thanks, Dad." Sandi refrained from pointing out that she'd called twice that morning to remind him she urgently needed to talk to him. With a touch of resignation she realized he'd only coincidentally had this time free.

"Well, what brings you to the studio at this hour?" he asked heartily. "We never really had a chance to talk about your trip to Rome. How was it, and how was Gabriella? Still as beautiful as ever, I expect."

He had clearly forgotten the purpose of her trip to Italy. "That's why I need to see you, Dad," she said patiently. "The fact is, Gabriella isn't very well. I spoke with her doctor while I was in Rome, and he told me she has gallstones that have caused a potentially severe infection of her gallbladder."

Richard's eyebrows rose in astonishment. "An infected gallbladder? Gabriella? I had no idea she went in for that sort of thing."

Sandi took a firm grip on herself. Since reaching adulthood, she had often wondered if all creative geniuses were as incapable of conducting normal conversations as her parents.

"Gallbladders aren't something you go in for, Dad. Everybody has one, even my mother. It stores bile from the liver, and it has to function properly or you get very sick. Mother urgently needs an operation, or she might . . . she might be in real danger."

"But Gabriella doesn't like hospitals," Richard said. "She never did. She even insisted on delivering you at home. And then we nearly lost you because the midwife was incompetent."

"Yes, Dad, I know." Sandi refused to be diverted into chatty reminiscences. "The thing is, Mother has finally agreed to fly over here to consult with an American doctor, but I'm afraid that when it comes to the point where she has to check into the hospital, she'll refuse to sign the necessary papers."

"It's certainly a problem," Richard agreed. "If there's anything I can do to help, kid . . . Gabriella's a fine actress. Hell to live with, of course, but a pro to her fingertips." A furrow appeared between his brows. "Sure is hard to imagine her with gallstones."

"Actually, there *is* something you can do to help, Dad. Mother pays more attention to you than she does to almost anybody else. If you tell her she needs to have this operation, there's a good chance she'll agree to have it.

She arrived in New York yesterday, and she's flying out here tomorrow. Will you come to the airport with me and try to convince her that she has to check into the hospital?"

"Why, sure thing, kid, it'll be a pleasure. I haven't seen Gabriella since my last wedding, so it'll be good to catch up on old times. Perhaps Linda would like to come to the airport as well. You know, to offer moral support and so on."

"Thanks, but I think it would probably be better if you and I went alone," Sandi said. She had no doubt that her father's offer had been well meant, so she tactfully refrained from pointing out that forty-six-year-old Gabriella was unlikely to feel morally supported by her former husband's twenty-four-year-old sixth wife.

"The plane lands at two-thirty. Can I pick you up here around two? I think Mother would rather ride in your limo than in my Toyota."

Richard readily agreed. "I hear you went out with Damion Tanner last night," he said as they strolled together toward his office door. "What did you think of him? He's a great guy, isn't he? Wait till you see what an outstanding performance he's turned in for *Floodtide*. I'd say he has another Oscar just about in the bag."

"How did you hear I'd been out with Damion?" Sandi asked agitatedly. "Did he tell you? What did he say?"

Richard stared at her in amazement. "Hey, kid, what's the big deal? Linda's analyst was eating at Ben's restaurant, and he happened to mention to her that he saw you both there."

"Oh, I see." Sandi turned away, embarrassed by her overreaction to her father's casual remark. She managed to produce a carefree smile. "We just had dinner together, that's all. Ben's food is very good, and I hadn't eaten there before."

"I was astonished when Linda told me Damion and you had been out together. I wouldn't think the two of you would have anything in common."

"I don't think we do," she said coolly. "Except that we both like ginger shrimp. Well, say hi to Linda, Dad, and I'll see you tomorrow."

A few seconds later Sandi decided that the fates were not being kind to her. By some horrible coincidence her father escorted her into the reception area at precisely the same moment that Damion Tanner walked in from the hallway. Sandi closed her eyes and cursed with silent fluency. When she opened them, Damion hadn't gone away.

He was wearing faded jeans and a nondescript cotton knit shirt, but the air around him seemed to crackle with electricity, drawing all eyes toward him. The typists, Sandi noted wryly, had all stopped working and were staring at him with wide-eyed appreciation. For her part, she concentrated hard on looking in the opposite direction.

"Hello, Damion," her father said. "Glad you made it up here in time for lunch. I have an interesting script I'd like to show you. How did things go in the costume department this morning?"

"Pretty well. At least three-quarters of the clothes fit."

Richard grimaced. "I'm not sure that's good news. Everything's working so smoothly, I keep wondering what terrible disaster is waiting to strike."

Damion's eyes gleamed with laughter. "Maybe you should know that my astrologer insists that my life is destined to undergo a cataclysmic change before the end of the month."

Richard groaned, and Damion chuckled as he turned to look at Sandi. The laughter faded from his lean features, and his eyes mocked her with their swift, sardonic appraisal.

"Good morning, Dr. Hawkins. What a happy coincidence to find you here! I was planning to call you this afternoon. I hope you slept well after I left you last night?"

She was painfully aware that at least a dozen people were listening to their conversation with undisguised fascination. She resisted the urge to tug at her skirt or smooth back her already immaculate hair.

"I slept very well, thank you," she said stiffly.

"Well, I sure am glad to hear that. About our appointment this evening, Dr. Hawkins—I plan to pick you up at seven o'clock at your apartment, if that's convenient?"

"But we don't have an appointment this evening!" she protested. "You know we don't!"

Damion reached into the back pocket of his jeans and extracted a tiny leather-bound notebook. "But I have it written down right here," he said. His dismay was so convincing that for a second or so Sandi actually wondered if she could have forgotten they'd made a date. She shook her head in disbelief when she realized just what she was thinking. Good grief, hadn't she realized yet that, despite whatever other qualities he lacked, Damion Tanner was an absolutely brilliant actor?

He extended his open notebook in her direction. His heart-tugging smile was reminiscent of a pathetic Oliver Twist begging for food. "Look," he said appealingly. "My secretary has it written down here in my calendar. It says distinctly, Dr. Hawkins, seven P.M. Dinner. Do you know, I told my astrologer all about you this morning, and he was very relieved to hear I was consulting you. What with the catacylsm looming ahead of me and all."

"God forbid that I should disappoint your astrologer," she said with heavy sarcasm. "After all, everybody knows how infallible astrologers are."

He beamed. "I knew you'd feel that way, Dr. Hawkins. I explained to him that even though you once studied astronomy you're not a skeptic about the enlightenment we can get from astral bodies. Not at all. In fact, I assured him you have a deep appreciation for the metaphysical significance of the heavens."

Sandi turned away, biting her lip to keep back a bubble of crazy laughter. Before she could compose her face, Damion had clasped her hand earnestly. "Thank you for agreeing to meet me tonight, Dr. Hawkins. I knew I could count on you."

Sandi sat down at her dressing table and stared angrily at her reflection. The sight was not very inspiring, and for a minute she considered changing her brown silk dress for something more exciting. Then she adjusted the skirt impatiently and concentrated on twisting her hair into a neat French knot. If she had a grain of sense, she would call Damion and tell him she wasn't going anywhere with him tonight. Or any other night, for that matter.

She had wasted a good part of the afternoon trying to persuade herself that she had accepted his invitation only because it would have been embarrassing to make a scene in front of her father's office staff. Unfortunately she had never been much good at deceiving herself, and she knew quite well that she could have refused the invitation if she'd made any real effort to do so.

I'm sorry, Mr. Tanner, but I have a previous engagement. I think your secretary must have been confused; I never make appointments after office hours.

That was all she needed to say, but she hadn't spoken the simple words. She had merely stood there, tacitly agreeing to meet him while her father watched in silent amazement.

She pushed her stool away from the mirror and stood up, flicking off the light without bothering to check her appearance. She had no interest in making herself attractive for Damion. She didn't care that last night he had thought she looked dressed for the convent and that tonight she looked even more drab. And she certainly didn't care that he had said her hair was beautiful.

Sandi marched into the living room and poured herself a glass of diet soda. This was positively the last time she was going to be manipulated by Damion Tanner, she decided, tossing ice cubes into her glass with reckless abandon. Nothing he had done over the past couple of days suggested that he was interested in anything more than winning his bet. The fact that his approach to her had been as much intellectual as physical simply underscored the sophistication of his technique. He was too clever to think that soft lights and mood music would do the trick, so he planned to seduce her with intriguing conversation. But tonight he was going to find her better prepared to defend herself. Tonight she was going to remember exactly what most Hollywood relationships were like: a couple of months (or weeks, or days) of blazing ecstasy, followed by far too many months of bitter recrimination and fading desire. Tonight, if he attempted to caress her body into sexual submission, he would be in for a surprise. She had finally realized exactly how she needed to handle him.

The intercom buzzed. "Mr. Damion Tanner is on his way up, Dr. Hawkins." The doorman, a devoted movie buff, sounded deferential. He was obviously impressed that this year's Academy Award winner had called on Sandi two nights in succession. If only he knew why, she thought with a touch of grim humor.

She opened her apartment door and waited for Damion to step out of the elevator. Tonight, she saw, he had given up his designer jeans and aviator sunglasses in favor of traditional evening clothes. His starched white shirt was completely plain, forming a stark contrast to the severe lines of his black dinner jacket and closely fitting trousers. For one crazy moment Sandi wished that she had worn something beautiful—some exotic gown in wild emerald green silk, perhaps. Then sanity returned, and she smiled her usual cool smile of greeting.

"You look very elegant tonight, Damion," she said lightly. "I'm impressed."

"I'm glad you approve. My astrologer told me that

tonight is a time for dignified understatement."

"I see. I'm almost afraid to ask where your astrologer suggested that we go for dinner."

He grinned. "Occasionally I feel very brave and make a decision without consulting him. It's chilly outside, so you'd better bring a warm jacket."

He hadn't answered her question, but she didn't push the issue. She was too busy wondering why, every time he smiled, her knees seemed to knock together.

A chauffeur-driven limousine waited for them downstairs, and Damion politely stood aside as she entered the huge car. They drove across town and ended up at a fashionable high-rise on a tree-lined street that Sandi recognized as the building Damion lived in.

She stared out the window. "Impressive," she said dryly. "It looks like an imitation Greek temple, but I don't see any sign of a restaurant."

"There isn't one," Damion replied casually. "I thought we could eat at my apartment tonight."

She feigned surprise, then said casually, "That's fine with me. You'll be just as resistible inside your apartment as you are in the front seat of your car, Damion."

"I know that," he said quietly. "This has nothing to do with our bet, Sandi. I wanted us to have a chance to get to know each other, and there aren't too many restaurants like Ben's where we can talk without interruption. Since the Academy Award nomination, I've found it difficult to enjoy eating out."

Stifling a brief feeling of empathy, she got out of the car and walked quickly ahead of him into the lobby of his apartment building, wishing fervently that he didn't have a talent for sounding so darn sincere. Although she knew it was all an act, he'd seemed genuinely wistful when he said he wanted to get to know her better.

They took the elevator to the penthouse floor where a maid dressed in a pink nylon uniform waited at the apartment door to take Sandi's jacket. She draped it over her arm and smiled warmly at Damion.

"Dinner's ready to serve whenever you want it, Mr. Tanner."

"Thanks. Are you ready to eat, Sandi? I'm starving. Your stepmother's on a diet, so for lunch we each had to order a green salad tossed with lemon juice."

The sooner they ate, Sandi thought, the sooner she would be free to leave. And surely after two dates, one of them spent right in Damion's apartment, she would be able to declare herself the undisputed winner of their ridiculous bet.

"Yes, let's eat now," she agreed. "I skipped lunch today, so an early dinner sounds like a great idea."

The dining room table was spread with a sumptuous array of hors d'oeuvres. The maid placed a bottle of white burgundy on the table and left the room.

"Do you employ a cook?" Sandi asked politely as they settled down to eat. "Everything looks delicious."

"No, I don't need one. I don't get the chance to eat home very often, and when I do, I enjoy cooking for myself. This meal is catered."

They discussed catering services as they sampled the hors d'oeuvres. The maid returned carrying a beautifully prepared main course of braised duckling and stuffed artichoke hearts. Their discussion turned to the relative merits of waterfront and hillside property and the difficulties of filming on location.

Despite its elegance, Sandi didn't much enjoy their meal. She had grown up surrounded by the luxurious trappings of Hollywood success, and fancy cooking had no particular appeal for her. As a small child she'd often eaten exotic foods like quail and venison and plovers' eggs, except when her mother was on a diet and she'd been forced to survive on whatever odds and ends she could find in the refrigerator.

Not surprisingly she'd discovered quite young that it was nearly always the company and the conversation, not the food, that made a meal memorable. Last night, even though Ben's cooking had been so good, it was Damion who had made the evening seem special. Tonight, however, he seemed distracted, as if his attention wasn't focused on the subjects they were discussing. She would have thought he was utterly bored if she hadn't chanced to look up and find his gaze fixed on her face with a curious, hungry intensity. His eyes held her captive for several tense seconds before she made some trivial remark and quickly looked away again.

The maid announced that coffee would be served in the sitting room, and Damion ushered Sandi into a small room furnished with a down-pillowed sofa and a low glass-topped table. One wall was covered with bookshelves, and the parquet floor was almost entirely hidden beneath thick Icelandic sheepskin rugs. A fire burned in the grate, infusing the paneled walls with a warm mahogany glow. The only other light came from a silk-shaded lamp tucked away in a far corner of the room. A Vivaldi concerto played softly on the concealed stereo.

Damion glanced toward her, then smiled faintly. "At least there isn't a mirror on the ceiling," he said. "And no incense burners."

"I assume you save that for your bedroom, along with the king-sized water bed and satin sheets."

"Would you care to come and check it out?" he asked softly.

"No, thank you." She sat down on the sofa, sinking into the billowing cushions. "It's quite late, Damion, and in a few minutes I'll have to think about getting home."

"Yes, that would probably be best." He turned and walked abruptly to the other side of the room. "Would you like a brandy with your coffee?"

"No, thanks." She watched him as he took a bottle from a wall cabinet and poured some brandy into a glass. She hadn't intended to make any effort at conversation, but almost against her will she heard herself say, "Tell me about your new movie, Damion."

"You mean *Night of the Falcon*, the one just now going into production?"

"No, I meant *Floodtide*. My father is very excited about it."

Damion sat down beside her on the sofa. "The filming went well," he said. "Your father did an absolutely brilliant job of directing, and the cast is good. But, to be honest, I'm not sure about the box office appeal. The middle section of the movie demands quite a lot from the audience."

"Is that necessarily bad? Sometimes I think Hollywood underestimates how much energy people are prepared to invest in watching a good movie. What's the main thrust of the story?"

"Superficially, nothing too complicated. It's about Brad Foster, a racing car driver who is framed for murder. Brad isn't used to thinking things through logically. He's accustomed to sitting in the driver's seat of a fast car and pressing down on the accelerator until he crosses the finish line, usually in first place. I guess you could say he's an arrogant man who exploits both the physical power and the sexual appeal of his body. When he's accused of murdering his ex-wife, he has to learn how to deal with a whole new set of situations at the same time that he's running for his life. Both the police and the bad guys are after him, and for the first time ever he needs to use his brains instead of his muscles. There's a woman who helps him, and all the usual chase scenes. There's also a very good surprise ending. But the real significance of the movie is that it shows a man in the process of discovering that he's somebody quite different from the person he thought he was."

"It sounds chock-full of box appeal to me. Does Brad fall in love with the woman who helps him?"

"Yes, he does." Damion swirled the brandy around in his glass, his expression suddenly introspective. "Sheila, the woman who helps Brad, is a lawyer. She's as intellectual as he is physical. But they make love one night in a hayloft, with state troopers practically pounding on the barn door, and the final scene of the movie shows them in bed, locked together in a passionate clinch. Your father is too clever a director to underscore that final scene with violins and a pink sunset, but the suggestion that Brad and Sheila will live happily ever after is made pretty explicit. Personally, I think the ending is totally unrealistic."

"Why?" she asked. "Don't you believe in happy endings?"

"Sure," he said. "I believe in most things that help boost box office receipts. You know the movie industry, Sandi, and you know that actors and directors can't afford to be too idealistic. Unless your most recent film made money, you can't raise the cash for your next project. So I'm all in favor of Brad and his lady lawyer living happily ever after, if that's what the studio thinks will play well on main street. But in the real world I'd lay heavy odds that Brad and Sheila would be heading for the divorce courts long before their first anniversary."

"Statistics aren't necessarily on your side," Sandi said quietly. "In real life marriages don't survive simply because the husband and wife are clones of each other. They last because two people decide to make a strong commitment to their marriage. In the very best and most loving relationships the husband and wife hold values in common, but they don't necessarily share each other's specific interests. Brad and Sheila may love each other enough to make the sort of lifetime commitment that a good marriage requires."

"Could be," Damion said cynically. "On the other hand, once the sexual thrill wears off, they may wake up one morning and wonder what the hell they're doing in bed together."

"That's certainly possible," she agreed. "What did

Brad find attractive about the lawyer in the first place? If she's so intellectual, why did he take her up into the hayloft and make passionate love to her?"

"Brad Foster makes love to any reasonably good-looking woman who happens to be in his vicinity."

She stared down at her cup of cold coffee, feeling her stomach give an inexplicable lurch. "A few minutes ago you said that *Floodtide* tells the story of Brad's character transformation. Now you say he makes love to Sheila out of habit."

Damion's mouth curved into a small, ironic smile. "Some habits are tougher to break than others, and being framed for murder doesn't seem to have much effect on Brad's libido. Besides, his motives aren't entirely clear, even to him. He's attracted to Sheila precisely because she isn't like all the other women he's known. She isn't interested in his body, and she certainly doesn't give any impression of being interested in his mind. She does seem interested in his career as a race car driver, but in an abstract, analytical way that infuriates him most of the time. He eventually finds himself obsessed with the need to attract her attention. He's certain, you see, that she's never experienced real sexual passion, and without quite knowing why he wants desperately to be the man who shows her what it's all about. He finds her indifference positively erotic after all the women who have begged him to make love."

She swallowed hard. "I see. How does he . . . why is Brad so certain Sheila's never known sexual passion? That's a pretty arrogant assumption, isn't it?"

Damion's gaze rested contemplatively on her lips, and she turned away to stir her coffee, ignoring the fact that it contained neither cream nor sugar. "I think you probably know the answer to your own question, Sandi," he said softly. "With your professional training you must be able to reel off the clichés as easily as I can. A man always knows when a woman is sexually unawakened."

She put her cup back on the table with a decided bang, slopping coffee into the saucer. "Maybe. But not every warm and passionate woman finds it necessary to dress in skintight red satin and walk around fluttering her eyelashes and licking her lips. There are more subtle ways of conveying sexual messages, you know."

He grinned. "Thank heavens for that!"

She breathed deeply, controlling an irrational spurt of anger. They were only talking about a movie, after all. There was no need for her to feel personally involved.

"I'm interested in Sheila," she said as soon as she had regained control of herself. "What were *her* motives for making love to Brad? It doesn't seem a very smart decision for a woman who's supposed to be an intelligent, well-educated professional."

"Doesn't it?" he asked neutrally. In the muted lamplight she noticed that his eyes suddenly seemed piercingly blue. He shrugged. "Only amateurs attempt to analyze the motivations of every character in a play," he said. "As an actor, I had to know everything I could about Brad, but I had no reason to understand Sheila's character. I just needed to react to it. You're a woman, so perhaps you can explain her motives better than I can. Why would somebody like Sheila decide to throw away years of self-discipline, knowing that she might get nothing in return except a single night of mindless passion? Knowing, in fact, that by her previous standards Brad wasn't a particularly worthwhile person?"

He had moved closer to her on the sofa, and now his body was so near that its warmth reached out to engulf her, like the heat that warned of an approaching forest fire.

"Perhaps Sheila is more passionate than she appears on the surface," Sandi said, swallowing hard to moisten her dry throat and staring at a patch of wall to the left of Damion's shoulder. "Perhaps Sheila senses the loneliness and frustration hidden behind Brad's macho exterior. Maybe she hopes that if they make love, she'll be able to touch him in some special way that he's never experienced before, despite all the other women he's taken to bed." Her voice shook just a little. "Maybe she thinks that, in his own way, Brad knows as little about making love as she does."

Damion's fingers insinuated themselves into her hair, and she made no protest as he slowly drew out the pins.

"Poor Brad," he murmured, letting the hairpins drop unheeded onto the floor. "Poor Sheila." As he trailed his hands down the narrow sleeves of her dress, she felt the heat of his fingertips burning through the thin silk. "I'm beginning to think that they really need each other," he murmured huskily. "They were lucky to find their hay-loft, don't you think?"

"I don't . . . know." She concentrated on breathing, which had suddenly become an amazingly difficult operation. "I haven't seen the movie," she said with a gasp.

"Neither have I. Maybe we could watch it together sometime."

He didn't appear to expect an answer, which was just as well, since her vocal chords seemed to have ceased functioning. His hands moved expertly amid the tumbled strands of her hair, his fingers exploring the exquisitely sensitive skin of her neck and his thumbs gently tracing the delicate line of her jaw. His eyes were bright with desire.

"We've spent hours alone together, and I haven't kissed you yet." His voice thickened with unexpected urgency. "Don't frustrate us both any longer, Sandi. You have a mouth made for kisses, and the image of it torments my dreams."

Her heart stopped pumping blood and began to pour liquid fire through her veins. Somewhere in the distant reaches of her mind she remembered that there were a dozen good reasons why she shouldn't listen to Damion's hypnotic words. She vaguely remembered that she'd devised some clever plan to deal with just this sort of situation. But at this precise moment neither the plan nor the reasons for escaping seemed important. The liquid fire had reached the farthest extremities of her body, and she let out her breath on a soft sigh, closing her eyes in a silent gesture of surrender.

He didn't pull her into his arms, but she moved against him, drawn by the demands of her own body. His breath was warm and brandy-scented as he bent to kiss her, and she trembled in pleasurable anticipation as his hand stroked down her spine. With agonizing slowness he pulled her hips closer to his body, letting her feel the full power of his arousal.

He traced the outline of her mouth with his tongue before parting her lips and deepening their kiss. The world began to spin around her, and the pressure of his mouth became the new center of her universe. She felt the ache of his hunger as if it were her own and moved her lips restlessly, yearning for more intimate contact.

As if he could read her thoughts, Damion reached behind her and, with practised ease, began to undo the long zipper at the back of her gown. Without breaking the passionate rhythm of their kiss, he pushed the sleeves away from her shoulders and lowered the tightly fitting dress to her waist. For a moment the air struck chill against her bare skin, but he quickly gathered her back into his arms, shielding her nakedness with the warmth of his own body.

His fingers trailed enticingly around the lace-trimmed edge of her bra, but he made no attempt to remove more of her clothes. The confidence of his gentle touch was erotic in the extreme, and the tiny ripples of excitement he created began to gather into an overwhelming wave, poised on the crest of a torrent of white foam. He was such an expert lover, Sandi thought dreamily. His sense of pace was superb, and he was obviously one of the very few men who knew that women required a lot more time than their partners to become fully aroused.

Her dreamy thoughts swam hazily into focus and began to crystallize, stark, solid, and unwelcome at the forefront of her mind. *Of course* Damion was a technically superb lover! Why wouldn't he be, when he was the graduate of an uncounted multitude of women's beds? *Of course* he knew exactly when she was ready to proceed to the next stage of their lovemaking. It wasn't because their minds were mystically in harmony. Damion merely had years of practice in picking up on the telltale signals of a woman's body. For the second time in two days he had managed to make her forget that he wasn't yearning to become her lover—he was merely anxious to win their bet.

The liquid fire running through her veins cooled down into ordinary, everyday blood, and her heart stopped trying to imitate a trip-hammer. She wasn't surprised when Damion—practiced, skillful, Damion—immediately sensed her withdrawal.

"What's wrong, Sandi?" he whispered huskily. "I didn't hurt you, did I?"

Not in the way you mean, she thought sadly. "Of course you didn't hurt me," she said lightly.

She edged away from him, slipping her arms back into the sleeves of her neat brown dress and quickly pulling up the zipper. With the dress in place she felt a little less vulnerable, but her hands were still shaking, so she hid them from Damion's view by rummaging among the sofa cushions, looking for her purse. Now, when it was almost too late, she remembered that she had worked out a fail-safe plan for coping with Damion's lovemaking. Nothing could turn a man off more surely than the suspicion that he'd appeared ridiculous.

She retrieved her purse and forced herself to look up at him, although she was careful to avoid meeting his eyes. "I was searching for my notebook," she said brightly. "Your lovemaking technique is so superb, Damion, that

I'd like to jot down a few notes. You remember that you agreed I could take some notes for the research paper I'm working on?"

"You want to take *notes?*" he asked. *"Now?"*

"Well, if you wouldn't mind too much, I can't think of a better time and place."

"What sort of notes did you have in mind?"

"Oh, they'd be very flattering, Damion, I assure you. Although, of course, in a scientific study, names and backgrounds are always disguised to protect people's privacy. So nobody would actually know for sure that it was you I was describing. It would be tremendously helpful if you could kiss me again, but sort of take the kiss step by step, if you understand what I mean. You have a unique way of placing your hands that makes it very comfortable for the woman."

"Comfortable!" he exclaimed.

"Well, yes. Would you believe I have one movie star in therapy who's so clumsy that he can never kiss his leading lady or his girl friend without bumping her nose? But when you started to kiss me I really felt able to relax and enjoy myself. I'm sure you could give me some useful hints to pass on."

Damion picked up his glass from the table and walked silently across the room to pour himself another brandy. He turned around to face her, leaning against the bar with the glass cradled between his hands. His features, she saw with a fleeting sense of loss, had once again settled into his habitual expression of faint mockery.

"My dear Sandi," he murmured. "How expertly you manage to cut a man down to size! Comfort, you know, isn't exactly what most of us superstuds are aiming for when we take a woman into our arms."

"No," she agreed, unable to control a sudden spurt of bitterness, "I guess mindless submission would be a great deal more gratifying to your ego."

For a moment his eyes seemed oddly desolate. "You

may find this hard to accept, Sandi, but intense mutual pleasure was more what I had in mind." He tossed back his brandy. "Would you like me to take you home now?"

"Is the studio limo still here?"

"Yes, I expect so."

"Then there's no need for you to come out again tonight, Damion. I've known the chauffeur who drove us here for ten years. Bill and I will do just fine together."

"As you wish." He sounded entirely indifferent to her decision. "The housekeeper will have put your jacket in the hall closet. We'll pick it up on our way out."

They exchanged only basic courtesies as they rode down to the lobby. Sandi watched the light inside the elevator flicking from floor to floor. In one fell swoop she had achieved her goals, she reflected bleakly. The chances of Damion calling her again must be close to zero, and for what it was worth, she could probably claim she had won their stupid bet.

She wondered why so much success had left her feeling so thoroughly miserable.

Chapter Seven

SANDI WATCHED AS Gabriella disembarked from the plane on the arm of the pilot, a stewardess carrying her flight bag following and two other members of the crew striding in front to clear a path.

Gabriella looked radiant, walking proof that life begins at forty. Whereas the passengers trailing behind her looked crumpled and harassed at the end of their long journey from New York, she looked elegant and serenely rested. She floated through the arrivals lounge, wafting delicate clouds of perfume and smiling with exquisite graciousness at everybody who recognized her.

Richard and Sandi were standing together at the gate. Gabriella, who invariably noticed men long before she noticed women, exclaimed with delight. "Richard darling! *Carissimo,* how are you?"

Despite their divorce, Richard was no more impervious to Gabriella's charm than any other man. He took her hands and raised them to his lips. "You're looking as magnificent as ever, my dear. Rome must have agreed with you."

"Rome always agrees with me," she said. "It is the world's most civilized city." She retrieved her hands and offered her cheek for his kiss, her eyelashes fluttering closed for a brief moment. "Darling Richard, these kind people have made my flight from New York simply wonderful."

Sandi watched her turn the full power of her smile on the captain, a man of around fifty who blushed tomato-red with pleasure and stammered something about how delighted he'd always be to fly a plane carrying Gabriella Barini. The copilot stood by, looking envious.

The stewardess, only slightly less dazzled than the men, held out Gabriella's flight bag. "Good-bye, Miss Barini. It's been a pleasure serving you. We hope you'll fly with us again."

"But of course." Gabriella extended her smile to the stewardess and then, needing somebody to hold her flight bag, finally noticed Sandi. "Dearest child!" she exclaimed, waving her hands vaguely. "So here you are! I wondered where you had got to."

Sandi was much too sensible to waste time pointing out that she'd been standing right there the whole time. "It's good to see you again, Mother," she said cheerfully. She kissed Gabriella's delicate pink cheek and took the flight bag from the stewardess. Her mother's hands were designed for fluttering and gesturing, not for practical tasks like carrying luggage.

They parted from the airline crew, and this time it was Richard who forged a path for Gabriella while Sandi hurried alongside carrying her mother's case. Gabriella concentrated—with considerable success—on looking beautiful.

They walked straight to the exit, not bothering to wait for the rest of Gabriella's luggage. Sandi had already arranged to have somebody from the studio come to collect it. Her father's chauffeur-driven limousine waited directly outside the main exit, and Gabriella greeted the driver with a kindly nod. She had difficulty remembering her daughter's birthday, but no trouble recalling enough personal details to charm her fans.

"Hello, Stanley, how are you today? And how are your wife and baby?"

"They're both very well, thanks. My little girl cut her first tooth yesterday."

"How very precocious of her! She is only seven months old or so, isn't she?"

"Six months last week, Miss Barini."

"Even better. Please give my best wishes to your wife."

"I'll do that, Miss Barini." The chauffeur opened the door. "It's a pleasure to have you back in town, Miss Barini."

Gabriella smiled charmingly and stepped into the custom-made Lincoln Continental. As soon as the door closed, she leaned back against the upholstery, expelling her breath on a sigh of pure exhaustion. Sandi looked at her mother's pale, fine-drawn features and bit her lip anxiously. The performance Gabriella had just given had cost every ounce of her willpower and most of her strength.

A sudden surge of white-hot anger swept through Sandi, shaking her with its force and unexpectedness. She had never before acknowledged just how much she resented her mother's obsessive dedication to playing the role of Gabriella Barini, worldwide superstar.

She forced the useless rage back inside her. After forty-six years of perfecting the role, Gabriella was unlikely to abandon it now.

"Do you want some water, Mother?" she asked. "There's some Perrier in the portable bar."

Hearing the coolness in her voice, she wondered why so few people recognized it for the disguise it was. The more turbulent her emotions, the more she felt the need to retreat behind a poised manner.

"Thank you," her mother said tiredly. "Just a little, and no ice."

Richard was visibly perturbed as he watched his ex-wife. "These gallstones are really getting to you; I can see that, Gabriella. You're whiter than a sheet."

It was not the wisest thing to have said. Gabriella dragged herself into an upright position. *"Dio mio,* Sandi, what nonsense have you been telling your father?" she asked angrily.

"I told him you had an infected gallbladder that needed to be removed."

"And I told you not to mention that dreadful word! Gallbladder, indeed! Is the last shred of my dignity to be torn from me? In Italian we say *vescica del fiele.* It is difficult to know which language is more revolting."

"Mother, you'll end up losing something more important than your dignity if you don't get your health problems attended to."

"She's right, Gabriella," Richard interjected. "Now, look, honey, I know you don't like hospitals, but the surgeons here in California include some of the most highly qualified specialists in the world. They can take care of a simple little problem like yours in half an hour."

"Ha! If the surgeon's knife does not slip, or the anesthetist does not fall asleep over his gas pumps!"

Richard removed the glass from Gabriella's hand and set it down on the specially designed table. "Honey, you're not behaving rationally. Anesthetists don't fall asleep on the job, and American surgeons perform thousands of operations every day. In only a tiny, insignificant percentage of those operations does something go wrong."

Gabriella smiled sadly. "Only one woman in many millions is as beautiful as I am and also able to act. I do not have much faith in statistics and percentages, Richard. It is the exceptions, you see, that are always most interesting."

Her father sighed, but Sandi was surprised and grateful

to see how patiently he continued to deal with Gabriella's fears. All the way to the hotel he held her hand and attempted to reason with her.

"Will you please think seriously about what I've said?" he asked, as the limo drew to a halt outside the Bel Air Hotel.

"Certainly, I will think about it," Gabriella replied. She squeezed Richard's hand in a gesture of thanks. "I'm grateful to you for your time and your concern," she said. "Perhaps I will have the operation, as you recommend. I do not think I would grow old gracefully, so perhaps it is my destiny to live only this long."

Sandi was shocked by her mother's response. Such helpless resignation was even less reassuring than Gabriella's previous obstinate defiance. She exchanged worried glances with her father.

"Do you want me to come up to the suite with you, kid?" Richard whispered as the chauffeur and two doormen escorted Gabriella into the hotel lobby. "I have a dinner date, but I can cancel it if you think I would be any help."

Sandi glanced worriedly toward her mother. The hotel manager was bowing over her hand, promising that no effort would be too great to ensure Miss Barini's pleasure and comfort.

"Thanks, Dad," Sandi said with sincere appreciation, "but I think maybe we've said enough for the time being."

Feeling her mother's gaze drift toward them, she deliberately smoothed out her frown and lowered her voice to be certain Gabriella couldn't hear. "I expect Mother will feel better after she's had a shower and changed into fresh clothes. She'll probably want to go to bed early."

"Yes," Richard agreed heartily, "a good night's sleep will do the trick. Well, keep in touch, kid. I'm glad you asked me to come to the airport."

Sandi regarded her father with a touch of rueful affection. Like his ex-wife, he preferred not to think about pain, hospitals, and surgeons if he could possibly avoid it, and he was obviously longing to escape now. He dropped an absentminded kiss in the region of Sandi's cheek and made an elaborate homage and farewell to Gabriella before retreating to his waiting limo.

Gabriella wafted across the lobby and halted at the bank of elevators. The assistant hotel manager pressed the call button, the senior bellboy held open the doors, and the manager announced that he would send a bottle of champagne up to Miss Barini's suite immediately. The staff members who couldn't find anything specific to do lined up neatly on either side of the elevator doors and looked ready for instant action.

But as soon as the bellboy closed the massive double doors of their suite, Gabriella's vibrant charm once again disappeared. Her face turned gray with fatigue as she sank into the nearest chair, covering her eyes wearily with her hand. She had lost weight even in the short time since Sandi had last seen her, and in repose her face appeared almost gaunt.

"Would you like me to order you a glass of skim milk?" Sandi asked, concealing her worry as best she could. "I don't suppose you ate anything on the plane."

"Milk is a cure for stomach ulcers, not for gallstones," Gabriella said, but she didn't protest when Sandi placed an order with room service, and she drank half the milk before pushing the glass away with a slight moue of distaste.

Her luggage arrived, delivered by one of the studio gofers, and the sight of her six Gucci suitcases seemed to stir Gabriella into renewed action.

"I will take a bath," she said. She gestured toward one of the pieces of luggage. "The clothes that I need are all in there, Sandi. Would you get me my robe, please?"

Sandi unpacked the robe and, while her mother was in the bathroom, busied herself unpacking the largest suitcases. She made a mental note to call the studio tomorrow morning to ask the personnel department to send over a maid for her mother. It had probably been close to twenty-five years since Gabriella had last hung up one of her own dresses, and Sandi knew she hadn't the faintest idea how to fill out a laundry list, much less cope with something as mundane as sewing on a button.

Her mother emerged from the bathroom looking somewhat revived, although Sandi wondered just how many signs of weariness had been concealed by the fresh layers of makeup. When questioned, Gabriella insisted irritably that she wasn't tired, but she wandered restlessly around the suite, unable to sit still or find anything to do. She snapped at Sandi's suggestion that they order dinner from room service.

"I am neither dead nor senile, Sandi, so there is no reason for me to hide in my room. In a minute I shall decide who will take me out to dinner tonight. It must be someone exciting, someone who will make me laugh. Antony Groves, perhaps? But he has become boring since he decided he was a reincarnation of Marie Antoinette."

"He doesn't belive in reincarnation anymore, Mother. Haven't you read his latest book? He claims that if we practice celibacy, sleep on the floor, and eat nothing but raw fish and bean curd, we can all live to be a hundred and fifty."

"Why would we wish to do anything so absurd?" Gabriella demanded. "What is the point of living for a hundred and fifty years if we can do nothing that is enjoyable?" She dismissed Antony with an impatient toss of her head. "What do you think about Grant Kopak? He has a wonderful mustache, and he always knows all the latest gossip."

Sandi concentrated on removing a speck of fluff from her gabardine skirt. "How would you like to have dinner with Damion Tanner?" she asked. "I could call him and see if he's free."

She was stunned when she realized what she'd just offered. She bit her lip anxiously, wishing a deep, yawning pit would open at her feet so she could throw herself in and hide comfortably in dark oblivion. Had she gone totally crazy during the last few days? Was it possible to have a midlife crisis at the age of twenty-eight?

Gabriella stopped her restless pacing and stared at her daughter. "Damion Tanner?" she said with far too much interest. "You mean the Damion Tanner who won the Oscar for his performance in *A Dream of Darkness?*"

"Er, yes. That's the one. But on second thought, it's probably not such a good idea. He may be busy or something, and anyway, I don't think you'd like him. He's very—um—arrogant. You know what actors are like."

Gabriella's gaze narrowed speculatively. For the first time since she had landed in Los Angeles she looked at her daughter with real attention.

"This Damion Tanner—he is your lover?"

"Of course not!" Sandi denied vehemently.

"No, of course he isn't," Gabriella agreed. She sighed sorrowfully. "It was foolish of me to ask. Naturally he could not be your lover. You look exactly the same as you have always looked."

Sandi's temper flared. "And just how do you imagine I'd look if I'd been to bed with Damion Tanner? Does sexual intercourse with him turn a woman purple or something?"

"I imagine not. But if his performance in *A Dream of Darkness* is anything to go by, a woman fortunate enough to be loved by him would not look as you do, Sandi. Her eyes would be a little less cool and a lot less innocent."

"Innocent about what?" Sandi cut off another angry retort in midstream and turned abruptly away. "This conversation is getting us nowhere, Mother."

"I'm not sure I agree. I find it most interesting. Please do call Damion Tanner. I would very much like to have dinner with him this evening."

Sandi walked reluctantly to the phone. The more she thought about it, the more disastrous her impulsive suggestion seemed. In the first place, there was almost no chance that Damion would be free three nights in a row. In the second place, even if he happened to be free, she must be virtually the last person in the world he wanted to entertain. And in the third place, she had absolutely no desire to spend any more time with him. That, surely, was what last night's little fiasco had been all about—a guaranteed method of ensuring that she would never have to see Damion again.

"I think we should call Scott Foreman instead," Sandi suggested, hoping she didn't sound as worried as she felt. "After all, he's the director of your next film and you've been in Rome since Christmas. You must have lots to talk about."

"Scott came to see me in New York," Gabriella said repressively. "In any case, I would much prefer to have dinner with Damion Tanner, so please call him. Scott is a good director, but he is a tedious man. Like your father. Perhaps it is in the nature of directors to be talented but boring."

Sandi didn't reply to her mother's comment. She dialed Richard Hawkin's office with shaking fingers and asked her father's secretary for Damion's phone number. Even more reluctantly she placed a call to Damion's home. She scarcely knew whether to be glad or sorry when he answered the phone himself.

"This is Damion Tanner."

She cleared her throat. "Er . . . hello, Damion. This is Sandi. Sandi Hawkins."

There was an infinitesimal pause. "Hello, Sandi."

His tone of voice was definitely not encouraging. "I was wondering . . ." She cleared her throat again. "Damion, I wondered if you would care to have dinner with me this evening."

There was another pause, longer than before. "Why? Do you need to make some more notes for your research paper?"

She closed her eyes. "No. The ... the research for my paper is all finished now. The reason I called ... I called because my mother is in town and she would very much like to meet you."

"I see." If she hadn't known better, she'd have suspected she detected the faintest trace of disappointment in those two curtly spoken words. "Naturally, I'd be delighted to meet Gabriella Barini. I've always considered your mother one of this century's truly great screen actresses."

"Thank you. It's kind of you to say so. Would you mind if we ate fairly soon? My mother's still working on East Coast time."

"Not at all. When and where shall I pick you both up?"

"I'm calling from the Bel Air Hotel, but I need to go back to my apartment to change. I could drive my mother to whatever restaurant you choose. Just say the time."

"I'll pick you up at your apartment at seven," he said. "We'll pick up your mother together, and if you like I'll make the dinner reservations."

She drew in a deep breath, hoping Gabriella wouldn't notice the heat flaming in her cheeks. "I'll wait downstairs in the lobby of my apartment building," she said. "And thank you, Damion. I know my mother is very much looking forward to having dinner with you."

"And how about you?" he murmured. "Are you looking forward to seeing me, Sandi?"

"Of course," she said with a coolness that belied her racing pulse and pounding heart. "You're a most entertaining companion, Damion. I'll see you at seven."

She hung up without waiting to hear his reply.

Sandi slipped her earrings into place and glanced quickly into the mirror. The delicate sprays of filigreed gold felt cool against her hot cheeks, and her neck looked unexpectedly fragile beneath the dark upsweep of her hair. She sprayed perfume around her shoulders, still looking in the mirror, although she wasn't sure what she expected to see. In high school she had realized she could never compete with her mother's sultry Mediterranean beauty, but she hoped that tonight she wouldn't be totally outshone. She had chosen a green silk dress that gleamed with iridescent fire when it caught the light, and her high-heeled black sandals emphasized the length of her legs and the slenderness of her ankles. She wrinkled her nose at her reflection, wondering why she was making such an uncharacteristic fuss over her appearance. Unless she draped herself in a potato sack, nobody was going to notice what she was wearing when she sat at a table with two superstars like Gabriella Barini and Damion Tanner. She picked up the silk coat that matched her dress and flipped off the bedroom light. It was time to stop making useless wishes and get downstairs.

Damion arrived less than a minute past seven. After so many years of dealing with Hollywood personalities whose sense of time was elastic in the extreme, his unfailing punctuality always surprised her.

"You look beautiful," he said quietly as he reached her side. "This is the first time I've seen you wearing something that isn't gray or beige."

In that instant she realized precisely why she had spent so long getting ready, and her reasons had nothing to do with Gabriella.

"Thank you," she said huskily. "I haven't worn this dress before, so I'm glad you like it." She flashed him a tiny smile. "I really appreciate your coming out on such short notice, Damion. Did your astrologer tell you to be kind to annoying new acquaintances or something?"

His gaze touched briefly on her mouth. "No," he said. "This was another one of those rare decisions that I made all by myself."

The chauffeur held open the car door, and they settled

into the back of the limousine. The seat was designed to accommodate four people, leaving at least two feet of padded leather between their bodies.

"I saw your father late this afternoon," Damion said. "He mentioned that Gabriella was in L.A. for a medical checkup. I hope there's nothing seriously wrong."

She hadn't intended to explain about her mother's need for surgery, but somehow she found herself pouring out the whole story. Damion was a quiet and attentive listener, and they were almost at the hotel before she finished her tale of woe.

"My mother is terrified of hospitals and surgeons," she concluded, "so I'd be very grateful if you could speak positively about the doctors here in California."

"I'll be happy to. And if your mother doesn't bring the subject up, maybe I can find some way to introduce it. Has Gabriella had bad experiences with hospitals in the past?"

"My grandmother—her mother—had a ruptured appendix and died on the operating table during one of the major battles of World War II. Gabriella was scarcely more than a toddler and the incident terrified her. To a young child it must have seemed as if one minute her mother was there and the next minute she'd been swallowed up by the hospital, never to emerge again. At almost the same time, the streets of their town had filled with soldiers, who were fighting house to house and sometimes hand to hand virtually outside her window. I'm sure my mother realizes that there's no similarity between hospital conditions in war-devastated Europe and those in peacetime California. But when she thinks about having an operation, she reacts like the frightened child she once was, not like a sensible adult."

"And, of course, her opposition is all the more difficult to overcome precisely because it's based on powerful emotions rather than on reason," Damion commented.

The limousine drew to a halt outside the hotel before he could say anything further, and they walked quickly through the lobby and took the elevator to Gabriella's suite.

Gabriella looked her most dazzling as she flung open the door and greeted them, her smile radiant, her thin body glittering in silver lamé, her throat and arms brilliant with diamonds. Knowing that her mother rarely felt entirely well nowadays, Sandi searched for the telltale signs of pain beneath Gabriella's makeup, but she could see none. When her mother threw herself into the role of superstar, not even illness could pierce her concentration.

Damion kissed Gabriella's hands, bowing over them with all the panache of a latter-day Errol Flynn. As he murmured a string of graceful compliments, Sandi saw that her mother literally glowed with pleasure.

"You have much to be proud of," Gabriella commented as Damion draped her white ermine stole around her shoulders. "Your performance in *A Dream of Darkness* was memorable. The development of your relationship with the heroine showed stunning technical expertise."

Sandi was surprised by the warmth of her mother's tone. Where her profession was concerned, Gabriella didn't bestow compliments lightly.

Damion actually blushed. "Thank you," he said. "Praise coming from you is certainly praise worth having."

Gabriella's eyes darkened with wry amusement. "Please don't look so deferential, Damion. I am not yet old enough to wish for handsome men to appear awestruck when they listen to me."

Damion laughed and clasped her hands to his lips again before offering his arm with a flourish. "The deference is only a disguise, dear Gabriella, for the passionate nature of my true feelings. I've made reservations for us at Ma Maison," he aded, naming one of the most expensive and fashionable restaurants in the city. "I thought you would enjoy eating there."

"It is my favorite place in Los Angeles," Gabriella acknowledged happily. "I hope there will be one or two people dining there besides the tourists."

Ma Maison turned out to be even more crowded than usual, and Sandi resigned herself to spending the sort of evening she had endured many times with her mother. As a teenager she had hated these "display" dinners with all the intensity of her young soul. Now she was mature enough to endure the circuslike atmosphere with no worse consequence than acute boredom and a splitting headache.

From the moment of their arrival at the restaurant Damion and Gabriella were the focus of attention, no mean achievement in a room filled with the famous and would-be famous. Their table, placed prominently in the center of the room, enabled them to see and be seen by virtually everybody. The maître d' poured complimentary champagne almost before they were seated, and the meal itself was punctuated by an endless stream of visitors to their table. Old acquaintances exclaimed loudly at the surprise and pleasure of encountering Gabriella or Damion, although Ma Maison was precisely the place where Hollywood personalities were most likely to run into one another.

Gabriella ate virtually nothing, Sandi noticed, although with the constant crush of people surrounding their table she probably couldn't have eaten much even if she'd been hungry. She drank one glass of champagne but no other alcohol. Sandi wasn't surprised. In situations like this, her mother quickly got high on all the attention she received and had no need for any other stimulants.

A famous TV producer left their table, and a middle-aged woman approached, her face flushed with timidity and eagerness. "Mr. Tanner? Damion Tanner? I'm sorry to disturb you, but could you . . . would you autograph this menu for me? I saw your movie, and I thought it was wonderful, and we watch all the reruns of your TV shows. My daughter has your poster hanging over her bed." The woman giggled breathlessly. "She'll be so envious when she finds out I've spoken to you in person!"

Damion's smile was only a little mechanical as he pushed away his fillet of sole and accepted the woman's menu. He'd been trying to eat his fish for the last half-hour, and Sandi knew that by now it must be stone cold.

"It's my pleasure," he said, scrawling his name for the tenth time that evening. He handed back the menu and gestured toward the other side of the table. "I'm sure you recognize my companion, Gabriella Barini. She's just arrived from Rome to start work on her new film. As you can imagine, it's a very exciting prospect for all of us."

It was the third time he had skillfully deflected a fan's attention away from himself and toward her mother, and Sandi appreciated his generosity. Gabriella needed all the adulation she could get to keep her mind off her pain.

The fan launched into a long conversation with her mother, and Sandi felt her gaze draw irresistibly toward Damion. The light from the table lamp burnished his dark hair with an ebony gleam, and in profile, his face betrayed an austere masculine beauty that she had never before allowed herself to notice. She watched as his lean fingers toyed with a bread stick, and she realized with a sense of overwhelming shock how much she wanted those fingers to caress her body.

He made a quick, unobtrusive gesture to summon the head waiter and murmured a brief instruction that Sandi couldn't hear. Underlings arrived to clear away the remains of their dinner, at the same time that the talkative fan finally departed.

"I've ordered coffee," Damion said. "Would anybody care for dessert?"

Gabriella shook her head. "Thank you, but I never eat dessert."

"I won't have anything either," Sandi said. "The meal

was delicious, Damion." She glanced covertly at her mother and saw lines of pain that even willpower and superb makeup could no longer conceal.

"I have a seven o'clock appointment tomorrow morning," she lied, "so I really need to get to bed early. Would you two mind leaving as soon as we've had coffee?"

"You've always had a tedious addiction to early nights and sober living," Gabriella said. "Still, I suppose it's too late to change your bad habits now."

"Oh, I'm not convinced that Sandi is irredeemable," Damion said casually. "In the last couple of days she's laughed at least three times when she didn't plan to." He leaned forward, his tone remaining conversational.

"Sandi tells me you have a slight health problem that needs to be taken care of, Gabriella. I understand you might need a surgeon. A good friend of mine was recently operated on for acute appendicitis, and the doctor left such a small scar that it's almost invisible. Would you like me to give you his name? He has an excellent reputation."

Gabriella's eyes darkened with anger. "Sandi talks too much about matters that don't concern her," she said harshly. "I do not plan to have an operation in the near future, so I do not need the name of your expert surgeon. Hospitals are not places for a civilized human being."

Damion took a sip of his coffee. "Your first movie was released in Italy," he said reflectively. "And your first American movie, with Richard Hawkins as the assistant director, was released a year later. How many movies have you made since then, Gabriella?"

Sandi glanced up, puzzled by the apparent change of subject.

"I've made fifteen movies," her mother replied. "Five in Europe and ten in the States."

"That's certainly an impressive record," Damion said. "What's more, you've built up an enviable reputation, not just as a star with box office appeal, but also as a professional who can be relied on to do the job. Despite differences of opinion with directors and with your fellow actors, you've never walked off the set. You've never held up crucial filming by throwing fits of artistic temperament, and you've never let your personal life interfere with turning in a top-notch, carefully crafted performance."

"That is what being a professional means," Gabriella said dryly.

"Yes," Damion agreed. "And that's why it's a shame that you're about to endanger your outstanding reputation."

Gabriella's gaze became icy, and she moved to get up. "Winning the Academy Award seems to have gone to your head, Damion. I think it is time for us to go home."

He reached across the table and touched her hand, urging her back into her seat. "Gabriella, forgive me, but I've admired your acting for many years, and your career is important to me. Very few people in our industry combine your natural talent with your capacity for long hours of dedicated work. You're an intelligent woman and strong enough to face up to some harsh, unpleasant truths. Acting is damned hard work. A difficult day on the set can drain more energy than a professional athlete's workout. Scott Foreman and a few hundred other people are depending on you to turn in the same high-quality performance on your next movie that you've turned in on every other movie you've made. But you and I both know they won't get it, Gabriella. You can't film day in and day out for three months when you're in pain. You can't do justice to your talent when you wake up each morning wondering if this is the day you're going to die."

Sandi drew in a sharp breath, but Gabriella merely glanced once at Damion, then looked away. "It seems that I have a delightful choice ahead of me," she said.

"I can die quickly on the operating table, or I can refuse to have surgery and die at my leisure."

"That isn't the choice you're facing," Damion said quietly. "Removing gallstones is a routine, low-risk surgical procedure, so the choice you have to make is between dying because of an irrational fear or overcoming that fear and living a long and healthy life. Knowing your professional reputation, I don't think you'll find the choice difficult."

Gabriella cradled her empty coffee cup with shaking fingers. "You have missed your vocation, Damion. You should be a politican. I have no doubt that you could persuade Alaskans to vote for a tax on snow."

He smiled. "Now there's an interesting new prospect for revenue enhancement! We should bring it to the President's attention." His voice softened. "What about it, Gabriella?"

She lifted her head, her chin tilted proudly. "I have a couple of weeks before filming begins on my next movie. There is no reason, I suppose, why I should not make an appointment with your friend's surgeon."

Damion raised her fingers to his lips. "Bravo, Gabriella," he said gently.

Chapter Eight

SANDI HALF EXPECTED her mother to renege on her promise, so she was pleasantly surprised when Gabriella kept her appointment with Dr. Matthews. She was even more surprised when her mother agreed to check into the hospital within forty-eight hours of the doctor's initial examination.

Unfortunately Gabriella's new meekness didn't mean that her fears were gone. She no longer bothered to deny the need for surgery, but she was still convinced she was destined to die on the operating table. She reluctantly admitted that Dr. Matthews seemed like a competent surgeon, but even in her more optimistic moments she obviously expected his knife to slip, leaving her so horribly scarred that no man would ever again desire her.

Sandi abandoned any hope of talking Gabriella out of her fears and simply did her best to alleviate her mother's anxieties by promising to spend all her free time at the hospital. Despite the pressure of work at the clinic, she volunteered to spend the night before Gabriella's operation sleeping on a cot in her mother's room, and Dr.

Matthews greeted her offer with visible relief. He prescribed sleeping pills, but Gabriella didn't sleep much that night, and Sandi felt close to exhaustion when she left the hospital soon after six the next morning. Her mother had greeted the nurses passively, lying silent and unmoving against the pillows as they began their preoperative routines. Gabriella's calmness was so unnatural that Sandi found it difficult to concentrate on the needs of her clients at the clinic. Despite all her years of professional self-discipline, she was haunted by the memory of her mother's white, stricken face and the sudden urgency of her parting words.

"Good-bye, Sandi," she had said. "I have not been a very good mother, but will you remember that, in my own way, as much as I can, I have always loved you?"

Sandi couldn't recall exactly what she had replied, but as she returned to the hospital at lunch time, she was obsessed by the feeling that her response had been inadequate. She was supposed to be a highly trained psychologist, she chastised herself, yet at a crucial moment she had let her mother down by not providing the reassurance she craved.

Sandi's worries were not eased by the message she received at the nurse's station. Miss Barini, she was informed, had gone into surgery on schedule, but she was still in the operating room. Nobody seemed willing to explain why she was still in surgery. Nobody even seemed willing to say how long a routine gallbladder operation normally lasted.

Sandi paced the waiting room, aware that the sick feeling in her stomach was caused at least partly by the fact that she had eaten neither breakfast nor lunch, and not much dinner the night before. She considered finding somewhere to buy a sandwich, but the mere thought of swallowing food made her stomach roil in revulsion. There was a coffee machine in the waiting room, and she helped herself to a cup of strong black coffee. It was at least the seventh cup she had had that day. The caffeine circulating in her system, she reflected wryly, would soon be enough to make an elephant jittery.

As she took another nervous swing around the small waiting room, some slight sound made her glance up, and she saw Damion standing silently in the doorway. He was wearing jeans and a casual leather jacket, and his eyes were hidden behind a large pair of sunglasses. Not aviator-style this time, she noticed abstractedly. Some of her coffee spilled, burning the back of her hand.

"Here, let me take that." He was at her side almost immediately, filling the dreary waiting room with the vibrant energy of his presence. If he was wearing the sunglasses as a disguise, she thought distractedly, somebody should tell him they didn't help much.

He set the cup down on a table and picked up a handful of paper napkins, wrapping one or two around her hand to mop up the coffee.

"Was it very hot?" he asked quietly, and she shook her head in denial.

He took her hand in his, pushing his sunglasses up on top of his head as he bent to examine the burn.

"Your skin's just a little red," he said, tossing the sodden napkins into a nearby wastebasket. "The damage doesn't seem serious."

"No, it's not even stinging. Thank you." She tried to get a grip on herself. "I was startled. I didn't expect to see you here, Damion."

"It occurred to me that you might need a little moral support."

She was dismayed by the pleasure she felt at his simple words. She had written to thank him for persuading Gabriella to see a doctor, but he hadn't replied to her brief note. In fact, since their dinner at Ma Maison he hadn't made any attempt to contact her, and she'd almost convinced herself that she didn't mind his silence.

"It's very good of you to come," she said stiltedly.

"How did you know my mother was having her operation today?"

"I stayed in touch with her," he said. "I guessed she might need a little encouragement to keep her appointments, and I knew she'd find it more difficult to chicken out on me than on you." He paused, then added, "A resident surgeon told me it will be at least another half-hour before there's any word from the operating room. Have you eaten lunch? Would you come and have a snack with me?"

She shook her head. "Thanks, Damion, but I don't think I could eat anything right now. Besides, if something happened . . . if the nurses had something to tell us, they wouldn't know where we were."

"We'll tell the nurses we're going to the cafeteria," he said, casually pulling his sunglasses back over his eyes. "Please come, Sandi. I'm really hungry, and I'd appreciate your company."

She agreed, since it seemed churlish to refuse when he'd been kind enough to take time out of his hectic schedule to come to the hospital. The cafeteria was in the basement, a cheerless cavernous space with orange plastic chairs illuminated by glaring neon strip lights. Damion loaded their tray with a big container of yogurt, a dish of vanilla ice cream, and two glasses of apple juice, then carried it to a relatively dark corner of the room. He adjusted his chair so that his back was toward the other occupants and stuck his sunglasses casually into his shirt pocket.

"You look tired," he said, pushing the carton of yogurt and a spoon in Sandi's direction. "I guess the past couple of days have been tough for you."

"They could have been worse," she said, beginning to eat the yogurt without really noticing what she was doing. "At least my mother finally agreed to have the operation, and that's been a load off my mind. Thanks again for your help, Damion. Gabriella wouldn't be in the hospital right now if it hadn't been for you."

"I think you're overestimating my influence," he said.

"Tell me, Sandi, has your mother always relied on you as much as she does nowadays?"

Sandi stared at him in stupefied silence, the spoon halfway to her mouth; then she laughed with real amusement. "Relied on me! Damion, for heaven's sake! My mother considers me only one stage removed from certifiable. She admires only two qualities in a woman— acting talent and the ability to attract exciting men. As far as she's concerned, I'm abysmally lacking in both areas."

"Then why did she summon you to Italy the minute the doctor there diagnosed her illness? And why did she come to California to have the operation?"

"I guess because she was scheduled to start work here on her movie."

"More likely because you're here, and you're the strongest, most reliable person she knows."

"Believe me, reliability isn't a quality that Gabriella yearns to possess," Sandi said without a trace of bitterness. She had accepted years ago that she and her mother valued different things, and the knowledge no longer hurt her. She smiled resignedly. "I doubt Gabriella would even recognize reliability if it came up and knocked on her door."

She had finished the yogurt, and Damion slid the empty container away, replacing it with the dish of vanilla ice cream. So far, despite his claim to be ravenous, he had taken only a couple of sips of juice.

"I've often wondered how couples end up producing children who are so different from themselves," Damion remarked.

"Gabriella blames my character entirely on my father's faulty genes. She's forever reminding me that my grandfather was a tax accountant. She firmly believes that all his bad qualities skipped a generation and resurfaced in me."

The corner of his mouth quirked upward. "Bad qualities?"

"Oh, you know. Fatal flaws like being organized and

punctual, and living in a tidy house. Not to mention a total inability to fall in and out of love at the drop of a hat."

"And Gabriella's genes aren't similarly tainted?"

"Heavens, no! Her grandfather didn't do anything much except stay on the family estate losing money, but her father was an opera singer, quite a famous one in his day. When he was angry, he used to storm through the house bellowing arias from Verdi's operas. On the other side of her family, her grandmother was a countess, known chiefly for the fabulous variety of her clothes and the even more fabulous variety of her lovers."

Laughter touched his eyes. "Clearly an impeccable lineage," he said. "Not a hint of practicality or common sense in two generations."

"From Gabriella's point of view that's eminently desirable," Sandi said dryly. "What about you, Damion? Did you inherit your acting talent from somebody in your family?"

"Not that I know of." He grinned ruefully. "My parents talk about actors pretty much the way your mother talks about accountants. If you listen to my dad, you get the impression that all movie stars resemble either drunken vagrants or aliens from Mars."

"That sounds like Gabriella talking about accountants," Sandi agreed with a laugh. "What does your father do for a living?"

"I grew up in White Rock, a small town in southern Ohio. My father is head of the physical education department at the local high school, and my mother teaches science there. They both believe that everything the human soul could possibly desire is available right in downtown White Rock. My childhood experiences were so narrow that it's difficult for me to imagine what it must have been like to be raised in Hollywood with two dynamic personalities like Gabriella Barini and Richard Hawkins for parents."

"It was very exciting," Sandi said flatly. "And however else you might describe it, definitely not narrow."

"That bad, huh?" His eyes gleamed with sympathetic understanding but, unable to handle his sympathy, she dug her spoon deep into the melting mound of ice cream in the dish in front of her.

"Why am I eating this?" she asked, suddenly noticing what she was doing. "Didn't you buy this for yourself?"

"No, I bought it for you. I guessed you hadn't eaten anything for a while." He continued speaking before she could protest further. "Where did you go to school, Sandi?"

"Oh, in various places. I attended everything from a small Catholic girls' boarding school to a public high school with three thousand students. My parents had a very flexible custody arrangement, chiefly based on whether my mother was in the process of taking a new lover or whether my father was in the process of getting married. Depending on the state of their love lives, I was either very much in demand or very much in the way."

Damion's expression didn't change, but somehow she knew her words had affected him. "Did your parents ever bother to find out if you were getting a decent education?" he asked. "Did they ever go to school functions or check your report cards, all that kind of thing?"

"Oh, yes," she said, managing to produce a carefree smile. "Gabriella occasionally floated in for some special occasion, looking divinely attractive and stopping traffic dead in the school corridors. And my father came to parent-teacher conferences if I called his secretary and asked her to remind him at hourly intervals. Neither of them was deliberately negligent, you know. They just always had more important things on their minds than whether I got an A or a C on my history term paper."

He grimaced. "Believe me, from my perspective that doesn't sound all bad. Unlike you, I had parents who thought school grades were the single most important thing in a teenager's life. I spent most of my high school years complaining that I wasn't allowed to breathe unless I asked permission first."

"I guess teenagers always want what they don't have. My favorite fantasy was to imagine arriving home late from school and having my parents ground me as a punishment. Of course they never did. For one thing they had no idea when I was supposed to get home. They could scarcely keep their own schedules in order, let alone mine."

"Did you rebel?" he asked. A hint of compassion touched his mouth. "In your situation a lot of kids would have slept around or done drugs in an effort to attract their parents' attention."

"I never got involved in either of those scenes." She stared at him, aware of a sudden, urgent need to confess the truth. "But I did rebel," she admitted, "by becoming the calmest and most highly organized person possible. I was the one person in my mother's household who *always* knew where everything was, the one person in my parents' circle who never showed any emotion. I was probably the only girl on campus who was still a virgin on her twenty-first birthday. I certainly must have been the only girl who stayed a virgin to annoy her mother!"

He suddenly covered her hand in a warm, firm clasp. "You don't have to be calm and organized with me, Sandi," he said softly. "When we're together you can be whatever you want to be." He touched his finger lightly against her cheek and smiled faintly. "But you know that, don't you?"

She stared at him, not trusting herself to reply because she realized suddenly just how badly she wanted to let all the barriers down. She wanted to relax the tightly held guard on her emotions and allow them to burst out of their restraints. She looked away, fixing her gaze on the glass of apple juice, frightened by the unfamiliar power of her own feelings.

He released her hand abruptly and leaned back in the chair. "My parents firmly believed that children couldn't be trusted to make important decisions," he said, and she was grateful for the casual shift in the direction of their conversation. "They even selected what classes I should take when I was in high school. The year I was a junior my father discovered that I'd signed up for violin lessons. His reaction was so violent I thought the poor guy was going to have a heart attack right in the principal's office."

Sandi laughed. "I can't imagine you with a violin, Damion. Do you still play? Or didn't you ever get beyond the squeaking stage?"

"I didn't even get as far as squeaking. My father considered violin lessons off limits for *his* son. As a phys. ed. instructor he thought real men spent their time building shoulder muscles and getting plastered with mud. The violin class and the football team both met for practice at the same time, so he simply recruited me to play football. I protested to the principal, but naturally he agreed that White Rock High School needed a fast running back a hell of a lot more than it needed a beginning violinist."

"He was probably right." Sandi's eyes twinkled. "And you needn't sound so sorry for yourself. I'll bet you made captain of the team in your senior year and had all the prettiest girls begging for your company. Have you ever heard of high school girls competing to date the lead violinist?"

"You're misreading my character again. Would you believe that I went out with only one girl all the time I was in high school?"

"No," she said, laughing. "Credulity can only stretch so far."

"Well, it's true. I started dating Janet Thompson when we were both sophomores, and I never dated anybody else."

"Janet?" Sandi glanced up quickly. "You mentioned once that your wife was named Janet."

He hesitated. "Yes, she was. Janet was very pretty, she was head cheerleader, and she was also the principal's daughter. With both of us having teachers for parents, we naturally gravitated to each other. She won a scholarship to a college in Cleveland, and I was accepted to Case Western Reserve on a partial scholarship to take a liberal arts major, so we left White Rock to travel to the big city together." The irony in his voice was unmistakable. "Our parents waved us onto the bus, none of them making any secret of the fact that they thought she would be the perfect wife for me."

"So you married her."

"Not quite as thoughtlessly as that, but almost." He shrugged slightly. "After we put on our production of *Macbeth*, Art Berenstein arranged for me to audition for a drama scholarship at the Film School here in L.A. I won the scholarship, but my parents wouldn't let me accept it."

"How could they stop you?"

"Teachers' salaries in White Rock aren't all that generous," he said, shifting restlessly on the hard chair. "My mother pointed out that they'd scrimped and saved for years to raise the money for my college tuition. They very much wanted me to graduate, and felt I owed it to them to finish my degree."

She could guess at the emotional blackmail that had been applied to him, even though he had scarcely hinted at it. "I don't quite understand what your stage career has to do with marrying Janet," she said.

Damion's voice sounded indifferent, but his eyes had acquired a definite glitter. "My choice of career has everything to do with it," he said tersely. "My parents felt that I was spending far too much time with 'undesirables' like Art Berenstein, and they decided that I needed a stabilizing influence to counterbalance my youthful fantasies of a career as an actor. They didn't have to think very long or hard before reaching the conclusion that Janet Thompson was the perfect solution. They admired everything about her. Here was a young woman of barely nineteen who knew *exactly* what she wanted to do with her life. She planned to become a kindergarten teacher in a small town somewhere in southern Ohio, preferably right in White Rock. She planned to marry a hometown boy as soon as possible and settle down, produce two-point-five children, and raise them exactly the same way she'd been raised."

Sandi sensed his bitterness without fully understanding it. "That's not a bad aim, Damion," she said. "Think of how many people deliberately turn their backs on the stress of big-city living nowadays. A lot of intelligent, talented people enjoy living in small midwestern towns."

"Sure. It's a great way of life—for my parents and for Janet, but not for me. Unfortunately everybody decided that I would participate in their plans without checking things out with me. Everybody agreed that I was the perfect candidate to marry Janet and father her children. One night when we'd been to a party together, Janet came up to my room, and we eventually ended up in bed together."

"Are you telling me she seduced you against your will, Damion?" Sandi murmured mockingly. "Did you go down fighting all the way?"

He laughed reluctantly. "A nineteen-year-old boy is *never* unwilling, Dr. Hawkins. You know that. Janet offered herself, and I took what she offered with extreme eagerness and an appalling lack of finesse. She was a virgin, of course, and when she came back a month later and told me she was pregnant, I saw no choice but to marry her. Her parents and mine were practically cheering on the sidelines. They couldn't organize the wedding ceremony fast enough."

Sandi drew in a sharp breath. "I didn't realize you had a child."

"I don't," he said. "Hell, Sandi, it's a familiar story,

and I'm not making excuses for myself. If Janet set me up, I probably deserved everything I got. I didn't love her, and I shouldn't have taken her to bed. I knew she was a virgin when she came up to my room, and I knew she wasn't using any birth control precautions. But like most kids that age, I didn't think much about the consequences. If I thought at all, I told myself there was no way Janet could get pregnant the first time she went to bed with a man."

"But I don't understand. Did she get pregnant or didn't she?"

"Who knows what really happened? I'm not sure I even care any more. All I know is that three weeks after our wedding she announced that—surprise, surprise—she wasn't expecting a baby after all. By then it was too late. We were married, and she had our future all mapped out for us. She told me she was more than willing to make concessions now that we were a married couple. She and my parents would have preferred that I teach science or English or some other sensible subject, but since I seemed obsessed by acting and the stage, they'd all agreed that when I graduated maybe I should look for a job as a high school drama coach. When I pointed out that small towns like White Rock didn't have drama coaches, she made the supreme sacrifice and agreed that I could look for a position in Cleveland. She made it quite clear, however, that she wasn't prepared to move out of Ohio."

"I guess Ohio must have qualities I've never heard about."

A faint smile touched his mouth. "It has beautiful trees," he said. "And Cleveland has a magnificent symphony orchestra."

"But not magnificent enough to keep you there?"

"No. Lots of cities have symphony orchestras, but there are only two cities in the States where you can really make it as an actor." His smile faded. "I went to

Art Berenstein late one night and poured out my woes. He was his usual ascerbic self, but in the end he stopped shouting long enough to pick up the phone and get me an audition for a role in that experimental Off-Off-Broadway play. When I was offered the part, I took it without consulting my parents. That may not seem like a big deal to you, but you have to remember that up until then I'd never made a single decision for myself."

"I suppose Janet was very upset."

"She cried for two days almost without stopping. I did ask her to come with me to New York, but she said the play sounded simply dreadful and was bound to fold within the first month. She said she'd be waiting for me when I came to my senses and returned to Ohio." He fell silent, then added, "She was quite right about the play folding, of course."

"But she wasn't right about you going back to Ohio," Sandi said quietly.

"No, I never went back. I stayed on in New York, supporting myself somewhat inadequately as a waiter while I haunted the theaters, trying to learn whatever I could about acting. I finally got a part in a decent play just about the same time Janet graduated from college. I tried to persuade her to take a teaching job in New York City, but she refused."

"Why did she marry you, Damion?"

His familiar, self-mocking mask was firmly in place. "Maybe because I was the first halfway presentable man who asked her. In retrospect our whole relationship seems amazingly impersonal. When she refused to join me in New York, she said she'd married me to have a partner who would help bring up her children in a nice home in a respectable neighborhood. She wasn't at all interested in starving in New York, which, as she pointed out firmly, was a city without any nice people in it at all."

Sandi touched his arm hesitantly. "You could never have made your marriage work, Damion. You and Janet had goals that were totally incompatible. You should stop feeling so guilty about what happened."

"I should also stop baring my soul to a trained psychologist," he said, his voice notably dry.

"I made that suggestion as a friend," she said. "Not as a psychologist."

"Is that what we are to each other?" he asked quietly. "Are we friends, Sandi?"

Something in the atmosphere changed, filling the space between them with an almost palpable awareness. A nurse came up to their tale, breaking a tension that Sandi was beginning to find unbearable.

"Dr. Hawkins?" the nurse inquired. "Dr. Matthews wanted you to know that your mother is out of surgery."

Sandi stood up, gripping the edge of the table for support. "Thank God! Was the operation . . . was everything successful?"

The nurse smiled a little too brightly. "Miss Barini is leaving the recovery room right now, Dr. Hawkins. She's doing real well. She recovered consciousness awhile ago, and her vital signs are excellent. But if you'd like to come upstairs, Dr. Matthews will be happy to talk with you before he goes home."

Sandi was only dimly aware of Damion's hand supporting her beneath her elbow. She knew only that she had to get upstairs before something terrible happened to her mother. She didn't need her professional training to warn her that the nurse was being distinctly evasive. She had known all along that her mother had been in the operating room far longer than she ought to have been.

Dr. Matthews greeted them outside her mother's private room. He looked tired, but cheerful.

"Hello, Sandi," he said, shaking her hand. "You look almost as exhausted as I feel. Sorry to have kept you and Damion waiting such a long time for news."

"How is my mother? Is she—"

"Right now your mother is absolutely fine, Sandi.

She's doing splendidly. But the fact is that she gave us all a bit of a scare. We'd run preliminary tests, of course, but when we actually administered the anesthetic, she had a somewhat adverse reaction. To be frank, there were a couple of sticky minutes there when we thought we might lose her."

Sandi had to moisten her lips before she could speak. "But you're quite sure she's all right now, Dr. Matthews?"

"I'm positive. Despite the trouble in the operating room, her post-op recovery is going even better than we could have expected."

"May I see her now?"

Sandi moved to enter her mother's room, but Dr. Matthews held out a hand to stop her. "I want to warn you about one thing before you go in," he said. "Your mother has a tube inserted in one nostril, as well as an IV running into her arm. The nasal tube and the drip are fairly standard procedures after an operation like this, but it can look frightening if you aren't expecting it." He patted Sandi encouragingly on the shoulder. "Listen, my dear, you have no cause to worry. It's a good thing she's sleeping, because I know she'd hate to hear me say it, but Gabriella Barini is a remarkably tough lady. She's going to pull through with flying colors."

Sandi shook her head as emotion overwhelmed her. "She isn't tough at all!" she cried, then astonished herself and the doctor by bursting into a flood of noisy, hiccuping sobs.

Damion stood very still for a moment; then he took her into his arms and pressed her face hard against his chest. He cradled her gently, stroking her hair until her sobs quieted to no more than a few shaky gulps.

"I'm sorry," she whispered into his shirt. "I don't know why I did that."

"Because you're exhausted," he said. "Because you love your mother." He crooked his finger under her chin and tilted up her face. "Let's go into Gabriella's room and take a quick look to make sure those tubes are dripping in the right direction. Then I'll drive you home. You need a good night's sleep."

She dashed the back of her hand across her eyes. "I need a tissue more," she said, sniffing.

"Here you are," Dr. Matthews interjected, obviously relieved that her tears had stopped. "In fact, here's a whole wad of them."

Sandi accepted the tissues and moved reluctantly out of Damion's arms. She wiped her eyes and blew her nose, then determinedly tucked a few stray wisps of hair back into her chignon. She opened the door of her mother's room and paused to look once more at Damion.

"Thank you," she said softly. "Thank you for everything."

Chapter Nine

THE DECISION NOT to see Sandi Hawkins was an easy one for Damion to make, and he had made it at least four times since he first met her. Unfortunately he had also discovered—four times—that although making the decision was easy, implementing it was considerably tougher. After Gabriella's surgery he had never intended to see Sandi again. And yet, here he was, about to drive to the clinic.

Damion frowned as he drove out of the garage. He was no longer sure how he felt about Sandi, yet his campaign to get her into his bed had once seemed so simple. He had planned a routine night of wining and dining in a good restaurant with no real attempt at seduction, followed the next night by a lavish meal in his apartment and a smooth transition into the welcoming embrace of his king-sized water bed.

The plan, or something similiar, had worked many times in the past. At the beginning of his career he'd been naive enough to assume that women fell into his bed because of his personal charms, but he'd soon grown wiser. He'd realized years ago that his professional success provided the necessary aphrodisiac. After a night in his arms women invariably complimented him on his fabulous prowess as a lover, but what really turned them on, Damion reflected cynically, was the knowledge that they were in bed with a superstar. He could probably lie on his back and stare at the ceiling, and his bedmate would go away convinced that she'd enjoyed a night of passion-filled ecstasy. His mouth quirked into a tiny, self-mocking grin. On reflection, that didn't sound like too heavy a problem to bear. Most people would be delighted simply to lie back and enjoy the fun. I must be getting old, he thought wryly. For some time now the emptiness of "the morning after" had threatened to outweigh the easy pleasures of "the night before."

He edged the car into the fast lane, trying to decide why his evenings with Sandi had run so infuriatingly outside the familiar pattern. What had gone wrong? Whenever she turned that elusive green gaze in his direction, why did he experience a gut-wrenching, primitive urge to throw her onto the nearest flat surface and make love to her until she cried out for him to possess her? Why did he want to talk to her—confide in her—as he had never wanted to talk to any other woman? Was it because she was such an intelligent listener? Or was it because he found her devastatingly attractive in her own cool way?

Damion swerved to avoid a car that had jumped lanes. Damn it, could he actually be thinking that Dr. Alessandra Hawkins was attractive? Apart from the evening they'd spent with Gabriella at Ma Maison, he'd never seen her when she wasn't dressed like a Central Casting candidate for the role of virgin schoolteacher. He'd never seen her with a single blouse button unfastened, let alone with an inviting display of cleavage. He suspected her definition of a sexy nightgown was something warm and cozy in pink flannel. He didn't even want to think about what she wore under those dreadful linen skirts. A chastity belt, maybe. In fact, all in all, she bore about as much resemblance to his usual bedmates as a marble statue.

The irony of the situation was that none of this mattered. Somehow, somewhere along the line, he had decided he desperately wanted to take Alessandra Hawkins to bed. Not because of their ridiculous, childish bet, but because he was slowly being driven crazy by the need to make love to her.

When he had called to set up their first date, he had spun one of his standard lines about imagining her hair spread out on his pillow. Since then his lies had come back to haunt him. For more nights now than he cared to remember he had been tormented by the image of her slender body entwined sinuously with his own. He had visualized her dark hair tumbling out of its sleek chignon and floating against his cheek. In his dreams he had tasted her mouth until it was soft with his kisses. He had heard her moan softly as he made love to her.

Damion felt his body freeze into stillness. *As he made love*. It was a long time since he'd thought of the sexual act as an act of love. His parents and his wife had taught him that to be loved meant to be devoured, to surrender every shred of personal and artistic integrity, and he resisted the idea of falling in love with every fiber of his being. In the three years since he'd left New York, he had come to know himself well, and he knew that he used sex as a way of avoiding intimacy. Taking a woman to bed meant sharing less of himself than spending the night talking to her. Going to bed with a woman meant he could join his body to hers while his mind and soul were tucked safely away behind their protective barriers.

But when he was with Sandi he couldn't hold his interest at a purely physical level. He kept experiencing the uncomfortable urge to reach out and touch her mind.

He wanted to discover the real woman he suspected was hidden behind her calm features, immaculate hairdo, and wrinkleproof clothes. He even found himself telling her things he had never told anybody else, simply for the pleasure of watching the enchantment of one of her rare smiles.

Damion steered the car into a parking spot in front of the clinic and got out, slamming the door with a satisfying bang. It was time for this idiotic mooning over Sandi to stop. It was one thing to want a woman sexually—after all, the chase could be all the more exciting for a little temporary frustration—but it was another thing altogether to find yourself worrying because that woman looked worn out from caring for her egotistical mother. And it was even worse when your stomach contracted with a peculiar, longing ache every time you remembered her folded in your arms, sobbing damply against your chest and asking between sniffs for a tissue.

He strode along the corridors of the clinic until he reached the door marked DR. ALESSANDRA HAWKINS. Sandi's secretary, a chubby, cheerful-looking woman of about thirty-five, greeted him with a breathless smile.

"Mr. Tanner, I'd have recognized you anywhere! Sandi said you'd be arriving about now, and she asked me to apologize for keeping you waiting. It's been a long day for us, and she's taking a minute or two to freshen up. She'll be right with you."

"No problem. I can wait."

Just as he finished speaking a door opened to his right, and Sandi came into the room. His heart slammed once against his chest and then resumed beating in a more or less normal rhythm. He leaned against the desk, feigning an indifference he certainly didn't feel.

She was wearing a brown linen skirt—again!—and a high-necked silk blouse buttoned to the side in vaguely cossack style. Apart from her hands, no skin was visible between her chin and her knees, yet all he could think about was how desirable she looked and how badly he wanted to see her stretched out on his bed while he slowly unfastened those damn rows of buttons.

"Hello, Damion," she said, greeting him with a pleasant smile that made him gnash his teeth in silent fury. Couldn't she look even a little bit excited to see him? Except when she worried about her mother, didn't she ever lose her cool?

"I'm so sorry," she continued, still with a polite smile. "Did I keep you waiting?"

"No. I just arrived." His manner seemed curt, but he couldn't help it. He wanted to say something amusing to lighten the mood, but his mind went totally blank as he watched her walk across the room, remove her jacket from the coat rack, and pick up her neat dark brown purse.

She draped the jacket over her arm and turned to the secretary. "I'll be in at seven-thirty on Monday morning, Glenna, to bring the paperwork up to date. Thanks for all the extra time you put in today. I really appreciate it."

"No problem. It's about time I missed a few lunches or I'm going to need a whole new wardrobe! Please give my best wishes to your mother, Sandi. It's great to know she's doing so well."

"I'll pass on the message," Sandi said as she opened her office door and walked into the corridor with Damion.

"I really appreciate your coming to pick me up, Damion," she said. Her voice expressed the same neutral courtesy she had shown to her secretary, and he looked away, resisting the crazy temptation to drag her into his arms and kiss her until she was hot, flushed, panting, and not even a little bit courteous.

"It's no bother to drive you to the hospital," he said. "I'm glad Gabriella feels ready to receive visitors. After all, it's only been a couple of days since her surgery."

"Yes, but my mother never likes to be ordinary." Sandi

blinked as they emerged into the late evening sunshine, and her laughter contained a hint of tolerant affection. "Since she didn't die on the operating table, she's determined to go to the opposite extreme and recover more quickly than anybody else who's ever submitted to the same surgical procedure."

"Dr. Hawkins! Dr. Hawkins! Wait! I have to see you!"

The shrill cry echoed across the parking lot, and a tall, angular woman ran in front of them, almost launching herself into Sandi's arms. She was gasping for breath, apparently from the effort of teetering across the asphalt on a pair of absurdly high-heeled boots. Her hair was short and orange, her face painted dead white, and her eyelids adorned with silver glitter. Her clothes were updated California punk, with a vicious metal-studded leather bracelet adorning her left arm.

"Thank God I found you, Dr. Hawkins! I was afraid you would've left for the weekend. I was afraid I wouldn't find you!"

Sandi patted the woman gently on the shoulder, totally ignoring the agitated swings of the metal-studded bracelet. "I'm here, Bernard, and you know I want to help. But you have to calm down and tell me what the problem is. Let's walk over to my friend's car so we won't be standing in the middle of the exit ramp. We don't want to get run over."

Bernard! Damion stole a closer look at the woman while trying to appear absorbed in crossing the parking lot. On second, closer examination he concluded that Bernard probably was indeed a man. His hands and feet were much larger than most women's, and his shoulders were considerably broader. But under the thick makeup his skin looked as soft as a young girl's.

"They were going to keep me in jail for the night until I said I was working with you. When I mentioned your name, the sergeant said I could come and talk to you."

"That's good, Bernard. Do you remember which precinct the sergeant came from? He probably knows me. Perhaps we've worked together before." Sandi appeared to have forgotten Damion's presence as she talked soothingly to her nearly hysterical patient. For a long time Bernard could only speak in babbling, garbled sentences, but eventually Sandi's sympathetic, matter-of-fact questioning produced the desired result. Calmed by her low, clear voice, he gradually relaxed enough to recount his story.

Bernard, Damion gathered, had had the misfortune to proposition a vice squad cop and, since he had several previous convictions for solicitation, the judge had refused to let him off with the usual fine. He was to return to court after the weekend, when the judge would consider whether or not to sentence him to a term in jail.

Sandi made no comment on the facts leading up to Bernard's arrest. She didn't ask why he'd propositioned a stranger or why he'd been in a bar that was notorious for its regular police raids. "When are you scheduled to appear in court again?" she asked, her voice not at all reproachful.

"Ten o'clock on Monday morning."

She grimaced slightly. "It could be worse, I suppose. Look, Bernard, I should be able to juggle my schedule so I can come with you. If you hurry, you'll catch my secretary before she leaves the office." She took a notebook out of her purse and quickly wrote a two-sentence message.

"Give that to Glenna, and she'll rearrange my appointments on Monday so I can come to the hearing and talk to the judge for you. I can't make any promises about what he'll decide, Bernard, but I'll certainly tell him that you've been working with me every week and that we've both seen a big improvement in the way you feel about yourself. I'll make certain the judge knows that you've never missed an appointment at the clinic. That's sure to be a point in your favor."

Bernard grabbed her hands pleadingly. "And you will tell him that I can't go to jail, won't you, Doctor?"

Sandi held his hand for a moment before gently extricating herself from his grip. "I can't do that, Bernard. But I'll tell the judge that, in my professional judgment, putting you in prison isn't going to help either you or the citizens of Los Angeles."

"Thanks, Doctor." He twisted his leather bracelet around his wrist. "I'm sorry about trying to pick up the cop an' all. I know we agreed I wouldn't go to that bar anymore." Bernard patted his orange hair in a pathetic attempt to restore his dignity. "Anyway, Doctor, I really appreciate your help. The judge'll listen to you, I know he will."

"You have my phone number, Bernard, and my answering service can always reach me. Call me over the weekend if you need me. If you think about going out to a bar again, please call me before you go."

"I promise, Dr. Hawkins."

Sandi watched his teetering departure with dark, troubled eyes.

"Hey," Damion said softly. "Why are you looking so worried? He'll probably only get a rap over the knuckles and a fine. At worst, he'll get a few weeks in jail. The prisons in Los Angeles are too crowded for the judge to keep him locked up for long. Is a couple of weeks behind bars really so tragic?"

She pulled herself together with a visible effort and got into the car. "For Bernard it would be," she said. Her voice shook with more emotion than Damion had ever heard her express. "He'll come out of prison with his deviant behavior pattern confirmed rather than cured. He'll be *more* likely to hang around bars propositioning people, not less."

"How are you trying to treat him?" Damion asked with real interest. "What's the first step? Persuading him to wear regular male clothing?"

"No, there's no way I could persuade Bernard to change the way he dresses. His clothes are his defense system against a world that's too threatening for him to cope with. All I can do in our therapy sessions is try to persuade him that there are people he can trust. He has to learn that he can make real friends, friends who will stand by him. When he has the confidence to enter into a permanent relationship, even if it's not a sexual one, then he'll stop propositioning strangers. Later on, if we're very lucky, he may decide that he's brave enough to throw off his fancy dress. But I've learned not to hope for too much."

They talked very little during the drive to the hospital. Sandi was clearly preoccupied, and Damion was content not to break the silence. Seeing Sandi in her professional role had cast her character in a whole new light. He was more than ever intrigued by the striking contrast between her superficially uptight personality and the generous, caring nature she expressed through her work. Bernard was one of the most bizarre transvestites Damion had ever seen, yet Sandi had accepted him without a hint of scorn or impatience. She had responded to him simply as a human being who needed her professional help. Bernard had expected to receive nothing but compassion and understanding from Sandi, and that was exactly what he'd been given. Damion found himself in the absurd position of almost envying Bernard.

At the hospital they saw that Gabriella was pale, with dark smudges of fatigue under her eyes, but all in all she looked remarkably well for a woman who'd just gone through major surgery. She announced that Dr. Matthews was planning to release her from the hospital within three days, and that she expected to start filming in three weeks, strictly on schedule.

Damion produced the gift he had brought her, a peach-colored organza bed jacket lavishly trimmed with marabou feathers. Gabriella thanked him graciously and allowed Sandi to drape it artistically around her shoulders. She still looked very pale against the garment's delicate peach color.

A nurse arrived carrying a dinner tray and Gabriella accepted her meal with a grimace of distaste. "My dears, you may as well go away," she said. "I shall have no energy to talk to you, even if you stay. These dragons disguised as nurses will hover over me until I have finished every mouthful of the revolting mixtures on this tray." She held up a bowl that contained something yellow and wobbly. "This is what they try to pretend is food!" she declaimed with some of her old spirit.

Damion grinned. "It *is* food, Gabriella. It's custard."

She shuddered dramatically. "It is not enough that I am nearly killed on the operating table. Now I must eat custard! I sometimes think there will be no end to my miseries."

"You have strawberry Jell-O as well," Sandi remarked comfortingly. "And a bowl of chicken broth."

Her mother did not deign to comment. "Good-bye, my dears. Go and eat something exciting, so that at least I can imagine you two enjoying your dinner, even if I must suffer."

As soon as they were in the elevator, Sandi smiled up at Damion. "I think she's well on the way to recovery, don't you?"

"It certainly seemed like it to me. Some of those shudders were vintage Gabriella."

"I wonder why she was so anxious to get rid of us," Sandi mused.

"You ought to know better than to try to fathom Gabriella's motives for doing anything," Damion said, laughing. He hesitated for a moment, knowing that the hesitation was ridiculous. He had intended all along to invite Sandi to spend the evening with him, and nothing had happened to make him change his mind. On the contrary.

"Would you like to come back to my apartment for

dinner?" he asked. "I was planning to make tacos, and I guarantee my recipe is the best this side of Mexico City."

"With an offer like that, how could I refuse?" She smiled, not one of her polite smiles, but the enchanting smile that came so rarely. He stared at her mouth, momentarily transfixed by the intensity of his desire to kiss her.

The fierceness of his need annoyed him, and he was frowning as he escorted her to the car. This obsession was becoming more ridiculous by the minute. The sooner he got her into bed and made love to her, the sooner he could get her out of his system and move on to more important things. He'd promised Richard Hawkins he'd read two scripts, yet he hadn't so much as glanced at either one of them. When a woman began to interfere with his work, it was past time to do something about her.

He let them into the apartment, then led Sandi into the kitchen. Nancy, the housekeeper, had left a note on the center cooking island saying that she was in her room if he needed anything.

He wadded the message into a ball and tossed it into the wastebasket. Nancy could enjoy a night off. He discovered to his surprise that he was looking forward with schoolboyish eagerness to impressing Sandi with his skill as a cook.

"Take a seat," he said, indicating one of the padded stools drawn up to the counter that separated the kitchen proper from the dining area. "What can I get you to drink?"

"After the day I had today, the smart move would be to drink ice water, in which case there's a chance I could manage to stay awake through dinner. Or I could have a double scotch on the rocks, which will probably put me straight under the table. But at least I'd go down smiling."

"How about compromising on a light Mexican beer?"

he suggested. "The alcohol content is pretty low, but it goes better with tacos than ice water."

"Sounds wonderful."

He took a bottle of beer out of the refrigerator, flipped off the cap, and handed it to her. She swallowed deeply and sighed with undisguised contentment.

"I feel more mellow already, Damion. I'm not going to offer to help. I'm just going to sit here, drinking beer and admiring your skill at the stove."

He pushed up the sleeves of his cotton sweater and washed his hands. "That's fine with me. But if I do all the work, you have to entertain me with scintillating conversation."

"Damion, I've been up since five this morning. Scintillating is a bit more than you can hope for. Even coherent is pushing it a bit."

"We'll talk about you, then; that should make it easier. A question-and-answer session." He chopped an onion and a green pepper with lightning speed, then tipped them into a pan. "For a start, tell me all about Peter."

"Peter?"

"Yes, your good friend Peter who travels a lot."

"Oh. That Peter. Well, I guess . . . I guess he's still traveling. I haven't seen him in a while."

A week ago he would have noticed no difference in her appearance or in her manner, but tonight he instantly spotted the faint blush that came and went along her high cheekbones, and he knew instinctively that she had picked up her beer because she was embarrassed and wanted something to do with her hands. He wondered why discussing Peter made her uneasy, and immediately felt a ridiculous flare of jealousy.

He crumbled ground beef into the simmering sauce and added a touch of salt. "Have you ever considered getting married?" he asked, surprising even himself by the question.

There was a short pause. "I was engaged once," she

said finally. "His name was Jim Bruckner. He was a psychology professor at UCLA. We called it off a month before the wedding."

"What went wrong?" he asked quietly.

"Nothing. Everything." She took another sip of beer. "Jim didn't really want to marry *me*. He wanted to marry Alessandra Hawkins, daughter of the world-famous director Richard Hawkins and the world-famous movie actress Gabriella Barini. It was my lifestyle that fascinated him, not me personally."

"I'm sorry," he said. "Finding that out must have hurt. But at least you realized the truth before you married him."

She looked slowly up at him, then said, "I think in both cases our pride was hurt more than our emotions. I've never admitted this to anyone before, but my motives weren't much better than Jim's. I wanted to marry him because he was a professor at UCLA, with a traditional family living cozily in the suburbs and two cute younger sisters who loved him and were delighted to welcome me into the family. If I'm honest with myself, I don't think I really fell in love with Jim as an individual any more than he really fell in love with me."

Damion felt a sudden fierce rush of emotion that he preferred not to examine too closely. He only knew that he wanted very badly to take her into his arms, to cradle her head on his shoulder and to feel her breath fanning lightly against his cheek. He turned abruptly and covered the pan of ground beef, lowering the heat to a slow simmer.

"We have to wait half an hour for this to cook," he said. "Are you starving?"

She shook her head.

"Then how about grabbing another cold beer and taking it into the den?" he suggested. "The sofa in there is a lot more comfortable than these bar stools."

"Sounds like a good idea," she said, the faintest trace

of huskiness lingering in her voice.

He led the way down the carpeted hallway, his mind a kaleidoscope of conflicting thoughts. Half an hour ago he had fully intended to seduce Sandi, but now he felt a confusing tenderness toward her that was more protective than sexual. Irritation flared again. He didn't like this constant seesawing of his emotions. Damn the woman!

"Make yourself at home," he said curtly, walking over to the stereo to put on a tape. He took his time digging out a new release of an old recording made by the Australian Seekers back in the late sixties. The crystal purity of the lead singer's voice seemed to fit his edgy mood. He clicked the tape into place, and a soft, haunting melody filled the room. He closed his eyes, listening to the first few bars, then finally turned around to look at Sandi.

She was standing absolutely still in the middle of the room, her hands clenched tightly around the unopened beer bottle, tension written in every tight line of her body.

Acting without conscious thought, he walked quickly across the room and unclasped her fingers from the bottle, putting it down on the glass coffee table.

"What is it?" he asked softly. "What's wrong, honey?" The endearment slipped out almost before he noticed it.

She closed her eyes. "I'm scared," she whispered. "I don't want to fall in love with you, Damion."

His heart started to pound so erratically that it was difficult to breathe. For some reason he was afraid to get too close to her, and he stopped short while they were still about a foot apart.

"You don't have to fall in love with me," he said. "I don't want to fall in love with you, either."

Fleetingly it occurred to him that this was rather strange reassurance to offer a woman he wanted to take to bed, but the thought vanished before he could fully grasp it.

"I'm not going to fall in love with you," she said, determination in her voice. "Just . . . just because I want to go to bed with you, it doesn't mean anything special."

He let his breath out very carefully. "Nothing special at all," he agreed.

She clasped her arms around her waist. "Lots of people have good sex together, and a week later they can't even remember each other's names. Sexual compatibility doesn't necessarily mean a thing."

"When we make love," he said softly, "it doesn't have to mean anything we don't want it to mean."

"Damion, it's crazy for us to make love! What we feel for each other is irrational."

"Irrational, maybe, but very powerful." Slowly he closed the gap between them, his movements gentle so that he wouldn't alarm her. He drew her against his chest, stroking the smooth twist of her hair. "Let me make love to you," he murmured. "Show me how I can pleasure you, Sandi."

Color flared in her cheeks. Her eyes drifted closed, and he felt her body tremble in his arms. "Tomorrow, we'll both regret this," she whispered.

He slid one hand caressingly down her spine, spreading possessive fingers over the slender curve of her hip as he pulled her against his thighs.

"That's how much I need you," he said thickly. "How could we regret something we both want so much?"

"Damion, this isn't sensible . . ."

"But it's going to feel so good," he murmured, reaching up to draw the pins from her chignon. Her hair tumbled down, floating in a dark, shimmering cloud around her shoulders.

He stared at her for a long, silent moment, then bent and carefully placed her hairpins on the coffee table. "If you really don't want us to make love, you'd better leave right now. If you stay, Sandi, I won't give you another chance to change your mind." He turned away, his mouth twisting ironically. "I won't be able to."

"I . . . want to stay."

In a tiny, faraway corner of his mind, Damion heard

the final notes of the song die away into silence, but the only sound he could hear clearly was the uneven rasp of his own breathing.

Without speaking he reached out to undo the first of the tiny pearl buttons at the high neckline of her blouse. Vaguely he noticed that his fingers were shaking. There were four other buttons on the collar and maybe a dozen more on the rest of the blouse. He was suddenly afraid he might not make it through them all without losing control and ripping the material. He had just enough sense of humor left to appreciate the absurdity of the situation. It had been a long time since he'd felt hard with need at the simple prospect of seeing a woman's bare throat.

His sense of humor vanished completely when the final button was undone. His midnight fantasies hadn't begun to do justice to the golden softness of Sandi's skin. Pushing the blouse from her shoulders, he let it fall unheeded on the floor as he leaned forward to kiss the vulnerable hollows of her throat. Her breasts were covered by only a filmy scrap of peach-colored lace, and desire seized him, exquisite in its urgency, painful in its intensity. He cupped her breasts with his hands, but the contact wasn't nearly intimate enough to satisfy him, and he moved quickly to possess her lips.

He had meant to be gentle. He had meant to take his time, drawing his lips temptingly over hers, demonstrating the wealth of his experience and the technical expertise of his kisses. But as soon as her mouth opened beneath his, he forgot everything he had ever learned in any other woman's arms. His tongue thrust immediately into her mouth, demanding her submission with a primitive male aggression he was powerless to contain.

If he retained any lingering trace of self-control, the eagerness of her response destroyed it. His tongue deepened its domination, and he drew her demandingly against his body, forcing her to acknowledge the strength and potency of his arousal. She shuddered within the tight circle of his arms, but her lips moved persuasively against him, and he knew it was desire, not fear, that caused her body to tremble.

His hands fumbled with the front clasp of her bra. In the past dozen years he had removed more articles of women's clothing than he cared to remember. He had whispered more seductive sweet nothings than he could ever hope to recall. But now his fingers felt clumsy, and his throat was too dry for speech. He finally unfastened her bra, and the wisps of material parted, revealing the firm, full swell of her breasts, pink-tipped in the lamplight.

His breath escaped in a long, harsh outpouring, and she stretched out her hand, drawing her forefinger tentatively along the rigid line of his jaw, pausing at the corner of his mouth. He opened his mouth, and her finger slipped inside, pressing suggestively against his tongue.

He closed his eyes, shaken by the fear that he might throw her on the floor and take her right where they stood. He drew her back into his arms, reaching for the hooks and zipper on her skirt. They came undone easily, thank God, and the skirt fell in a little heap at her ankles.

He realized then that they were still standing in the middle of the room, and he picked her up to carry her over to the sofa. Her body felt light and soft in his arms, and she didn't resist as he lowered her onto the pillows and swiftly removed the remainder of their clothes. Kneeling beside her, he touched his mouth to her stomach, teasing a slow, moist trail of kisses all the way to her breasts. He circled her nipples rhythmically with the tips of his fingers, resisting the urge to suckle her breasts until he was sure she was ready for the caress.

She moaned softly as he finally closed his mouth over the swollen peaks his touch had created, and he felt her pleasure as if it were his own. She reached out, pulling him toward her, pressing her mouth urgently against his.

He could feel her heart beating wildly against his chest. He slipped his hands between her thighs, teasing them open as his mouth moved tenderly along the length of her body. At the touch of his fingers she gave a tiny startled gasp, and he looked up quickly, afraid that he might somehow have hurt her.

But he saw at once that she hadn't gasped from pain. Her lips were wet from their kisses, and her hair was tangled in a wild mass around her face. Her green eyes— the cool eyes that had tormented so many of his dreams— were cool no longer. Drugged and heavy-lidded with desire, they gazed at him with all the passion he had ever longed to see.

She stirred restlessly against the puffy cushions of the sofa, moving as if the velvet irritated her skin.

"I want you, Damion," she said huskily. "I . . . need you. Please don't wait any longer."

For an instant he felt a familiar surge of male triumph leap through his body, the familiar gratification that came from knowing a woman wanted him to possess her. Then the triumph faded, to be replaced by a nameless yearning, a longing so intense that it was physically painful. He wanted to say something to Sandi, something that would let her know his feelings for her were special—that this lovemaking was different from anything he had experienced before. With a shattering sense of self-discovery, he realized he wanted to say he loved her.

I love you, Sandi. The simple words formed in his mind, but his vocal chords refused to produce them. His tongue felt thick and awkward inside his mouth. He had told many women he loved them, but he had never once meant it. Now, when the words were true, he found he couldn't speak them.

"I want you more than I ever thought I could want any woman," he said huskily. "You're beautiful, Sandi." Crazy, inadequate words to express what he was feeling!

"Make love to me, Damion. Now." Her body quivered

beneath the touch of his hand, enticing and promising all at once. He kissed her lingeringly as he eased himself down on top of her.

Her dark warmth sealed around him, relieving the aching pressure in his loins. He moved slowly at first, forcing himself to control the rhythm of his possession until she thrust upward with her hips, murmuring his name.

His desire grew until it consumed him, an agonizing need demanding release. He thrust harder, and Sandi cried out, her body beginning to shudder in his arms.

He held her close, his mouth covering hers as he drank in the small sounds of her pleasure. She arched against him in one final convulsive movement, her softness dissolving inextricably into his power.

The last vestiges of his self-control vanished. The pressure in his loins exploded, breaking apart in a tumultuous burst of indescribable ecstasy. He was no longer sure whether he felt agony or joy; he knew only that he had never before felt anything so intense.

Later, much later, he raised himself on one elbow and looked down at Sandi. Sweat had matted a lock of hair to her forehead, and he pushed it out of her eyes with a surge of inexplicable tenderness. Her cheeks were still flushed with the afterglow of their passion, and he thought that he had never seen anyone look so beautiful.

She glanced up, her eyes bright and unfathomable. "Damion..." she murmured.

He touched his finger to her swollen lips. "Thank you," he said softly. "For making love to me."

Chapter Ten

SUNLIGHT POURING THROUGH a chink in the heavy drapes woke Sandi early the next morning. For a moment she lay still, luxuriating in the feel of Damion's hard, lean body pressed close to her own. His water bed was custom made and larger than king sized but, despite all the space, they were curled up against each other in the middle of the bed, his arm flung out to rest with casual possession on her hip, her head pillowed on his shoulder.

She moved stealthily so that she could look at his face more closely. He didn't seem very relaxed, she thought. Even in sleep faint shadows darkened the tanned skin beneath his eyes, and the lines of weariness about his mouth hadn't entirely disappeared. Her heart ached with a longing to reach out, to gather him into her arms and kiss away his tension.

She closed her eyes, deliberately resisting the urge. She wouldn't let herself fall into the trap of thinking she was the one woman in the world who could erase those harsh lines and smooth out the knots of strain from his body. She wouldn't deceive herself into thinking that last night had been as special for Damion as it had been for her.

She had been right to be scared of making love to him, Sandi thought, opening her eyes and staring at the narrow beam of sunlight dancing on the bedcovers. Some wise feminine instinct had warned her that to make love with Damion would be to risk everything she valued, everything that made her life secure. And her instincts had proven infallible. Her response to his lovemaking had been shattering in its emotional intensity and frightening in its sheer physical passion. Her professional training had taught her everything about the theory of sexual relationships, but last night with Damion she had learned for the first time what it meant to make love.

And now she was running really scared.

Panic washed over her in a heated wave. She had always sworn that she would never love anyone until she knew he loved her in return. She had always sworn she would never allow herself to become emotionally involved with an actor. As a child, she'd learned many times from Gabriella and Richard that actors reserved their real emotions for the camera, and she had shaped her life accordingly. Having spent her childhood as a very poor second to the camera lens, she had no intention of spending her adult life the same way.

Damion stirred in his sleep, and Sandi seized the opportunity to slip her head off his arm. She moved to the edge of the bed, knowing she really ought to get up. She couldn't afford to make love with Damion again; it was too threatening. She couldn't afford to feel tenderness for him or any of the softer emotions. Damion was a professional actor, dedicated to a demanding and soul-consuming profession, and she knew he had no time in his hectic schedule for a permanent relationship. For superstars like Damion, she reminded herself, falling in love was like an absorbing hobby, an activity that entertained him in the slack moments between movies. Whereas she, Dr. Alessandra Hawkins, was a sensible woman who had no room in her life for casual sex and meaningless affairs.

Sandi pleated the cream wool blanket between nervous fingers and tried to remember why it was so important to be sensible. She mentally listed seven excellent reasons why casual sex was bad for someone like her. If she got up right now, maybe she could leave the apartment before Damion woke up. On the other hand, if she stayed in bed, maybe he would make love to her just one more time. She stared defiantly at the bunched-up blanket. Surely even sensible women were entitled to a once-in-a-lifetime morning of recklessness?

She was so lost in depressing thoughts that the touch of Damion's hand against her cheek startled her.

"Well, hello there," he said softly, propping himself up on one elbow.

"Hi."

"How come you're so far away from me?" he asked huskily. "We fitted so well together in the middle of the bed."

"I was about to get up."

He glanced at her searchingly, a hint of sympathetic understanding lurking behind the mockery of his brilliant blue eyes. He crooked his finger under her chin and gently lifted her face for his inspection.

"Hey, what is this? How come you're looking sad and gloomy when you're lying in my super-deluxe, hand-crafted, temperature-controlled water bed? Did I forget to tell you that sad faces are strictly against house rules?"

She wriggled a little closer to the edge of the bed and managed to produce a smile. "I'm sulking because you don't have black satin sheets," she said lightly. "Every superstud is supposed to have them."

He grinned. "You should have told me before we went

to bed last night. I don't take my duties as a superstud lightly, you know, and I have several sets in the linen closet. When I lived in New York and my TV series had just hit number one in the ratings, they seemed to fit with my self-image." He absently ran his fingers over the blue percale sheet and up onto her stomach. "I think I've grown up since then," he added quietly.

His fingers trailed around her stomach in lazy, erratic circles. Unthinkingly she placed her hands on his tanned chest, stroking the mat of springy dark hair beneath her fingers. "Didn't you ever fall in love, Damion, during all those years you spent in New York?"

His eyes gleamed with sardonic humor. "Certainly I fell in love," he said. "You're the most ego-deflating woman, Sandi. Haven't you read *any* of my publicity?"

"I didn't ask how many starlets you'd bedded on black satin. I asked if you'd ever fallen in love. Really in love."

For an instant his expression was shuttered; then he shrugged. "No," he said coolly. "I never did."

He leaned toward her, his expression disguised by the pattern of light and shadow cast by the narrow beam of sunlight.

"What about you, Sandi? Have you ever been in love?"

Not until I met you, she thought. She squeezed her eyes shut, pushing the treacherous knowledge away. "No," she said. "No, I've never really fallen in love."

He was so close now that she could feel the strong, steady beat of his heart against her bare breasts. What was he thinking as he looked at her? They had spent half the night making love, but he had never once suggested that he wanted anything more than the temporary pleasure of possessing her body. Did he really see *her*, she wondered, or was she just one more in an endless parade of women? She twisted her head on the pillow, looking away before he could see the desolation in her eyes.

"Sandi . . . don't turn away . . ." His voice was unexpectedly hesitant. "I want you. Please. I want us to make love again."

"It's getting late. I ought to leave."

"Not yet," he whispered.

As his lips pressed against the side of her neck, the stubble of his beard lightly scraped her skin. She shivered inwardly as he caught her wrist, pulling her near even as she tried to lean away from him. They both knew she wasn't seriously trying to escape. Making love to Damion had proven a dangerous pastime, cruelly addictive in its pleasures. How could she deny herself something she wanted so badly? She realized despairingly that she was only pretending reluctance to salve her conscience and make the joy of his conquest all the sweeter.

"You're so beautiful, Sandi," he murmured. Hungrily his lips touched her hair, her eyes, her face, before turning to her mouth as if he were starving for the taste of it.

She made a token effort to evade him, but he ignored her resistance, cupping her face in his hands and kissing her anyway. For a moment she kept her lips closed, but his hands stroked down her body and circled masterfully inside her thighs. He had learned last night exactly how to arouse her, and he remembered his lessons all too well. His fingers teased her to immediate white-hot readiness, and she opened her mouth on a gasp of insidious longing.

She clutched her hands around his neck, drinking in his kiss. Her body was weightless, melting into Damion's, and her bones slowly dissolved into liquid fire. Why had none of her physiology textbooks ever discussed these interesting scientific phenomena? Surely something as strange as liquid bones deserved at least a footnote, she thought dreamily.

He caressed her until she was blind and deaf with need for him. Her universe shrank until it contained nothing except the taste of him on her lips and the touch of him against her skin. His breath seared her cheek as he moved on top of her, filling the aching void within. Her body welcomed his presence, shuddering with delight as he moved inside her with a raw, thrusting urgency that demanded her ultimate response.

The ache of her desire intensified until she dug her fingernails into his back and arched her body upward in a silent, desperate plea for release.

"I love you, Sandi," he said, and she cried out as her body shattered into a million star-points of ecstasy.

She must have fallen asleep again, or perhaps she didn't hear the buzz of the doorbell simply because Damion's bedroom was at the far end of his apartment. Whatever the reason, she was dozing, less than half awake, when a quick tap sounded on the bedroom door. There was barely time to pull the sheet up to her shoulders before the housekeeper entered the room.

"Oh, I'm sorry, Mr. Tanner. I thought you were alone. I didn't realize you brought somebody home with you last night." The housekeeper seemed neither embarrassed nor unduly surprised to find her employer tucked up in his water bed with an unidentified young woman.

"Good morning, miss," she added politely to Sandi, without really bothering to look at her. Women in Damion Tanner's bed obviously fell into a generic category as far as she was concerned. She turned her attention back to Damion.

"Mr. Richard Hawkins is here, Mr. Tanner. Should I ask him to wait?"

"Yes, that would definitely be a good—"

"Like hell I'm going to wait," Richard's voice boomed out from the corridor. "I've been waiting ten days already for you to read this damned script, and the first option runs out tomorrow."

The housekeeper tactfully disappeared as Richard strode into the dimly lit bedroom and walked to the windows, not looking at the bed.

"Good Lord almighty, Damion, it's almost noon." He pulled back the drapes, flooding the bedroom with sunlight. "Get rid of your popsie, and let's get on with some work. We have less than twenty-four hours to decide whether we're going to shell out another half-million dollars, and so far you haven't even read the damn script."

Richard swung around and finally took a good look at the bed. Just in time, Sandi pulled the blue percale sheet over her head and prayed fervently for an earthquake. Perhaps in the resulting confusion she could escape from the bedroom without her father recognizing her. Her faint hope vanished as soon as Damion spoke.

"This isn't a popsie," he said coolly, presumably seeing no reason to keep her identity secret. "This is Sandi."

She felt herself blush from her scalp all the way down to the soles of her feet. As far as she could see from her perspective underneath the bedclothes, her entire skin had turned an interesting shade somewhere between fuschia and dark puce.

"I don't care what the heck her name—" A choking noise halted Richard in midsentence. "You mean *my daughter* Sandi is in bed with you? Sandi Hawkins? But why in the world would you take Sandi to bed?"

Damion didn't reply, probably out of consideration for her pride, Sandi reflected bleakly. She hated to think how he would have answered her father's question if the two men had been alone. She lowered the top sheet to the level of her nose.

"Er, hello, Dad."

Her father looked at her once, then glanced away. "Good morning," he said curtly. His voice died away into silence. He cleared his throat several times.

"What the devil are you doing taking Sandi to bed?" He repeated to Damion, but his tone still conveyed astonishment at Damion's choosing to do something so strange, rather than outrage at his daughter's being seduced.

"If you'd leave so Sandi and I can get dressed, maybe we could talk about this later."

"Well, okay," Richard grunted reluctantly. "But remember we're running short of time here, so for godsake don't start playing funny games in the shower. Where's your copy of the script?"

"On the coffee table in the living room."

"I'll go get it, and then I'm coming back in here, so you'd better get your act in gear, Damion. I can't believe it! Taking Sandi to bed when you have a script to read!" He marched out of the room, slamming the door behind him.

The hall carpet swallowed up the sound of his footsteps, making the bedroom oppressively silent.

"I'm sorry about that," Damion said quietly. "Nancy, my housekeeper, would never have let anybody in if she'd known I had ... company."

"No, I'm sure Nancy is superbly trained." Sandi got up, wrapping herself in the top sheet. Logically speaking it was a bit late for modesty, but right now she wasn't feeling very logical, whereas Damion was handling the situation with all of his usual aplomb. He didn't seem at all embarrassed by the more farcical elements of their position. Perhaps that wasn't so surprising. Barring one or two original twists, she reflected bitterly, it was no doubt a scene he had played many times before.

"I want to take a shower," she said flatly, avoiding Damion's gaze.

"There are two bathrooms connected to this bedroom," he said, gesturing toward a series of white-paneled doors set into the far wall. "I usually shower in the one to the right of that mirror, so you can take the one to the left."

"His and her bathrooms," she said tightly. "How convenient for getting rid of last night's indiscretions promptly!"

"Yes, if that's what I want to do, it's very convenient." There was a moment's pause. "Sandi, this isn't the moment to talk about last night. Your father's waiting for me to read that script—"

"Please don't worry about a thing," she interrupted, walking toward the bathroom. She was so angry and hurt she could hardly see straight. "I was born in Hollywood, and I know options on a hot script take precedence over discussions with last night's popsie."

"A million-dollar option on a script takes precedence over a lot of things," he said tersely. "But that isn't why I said this wasn't the right time to talk."

Having reached the bathroom, she groped for the door handle, keeping her back turned to him so he wouldn't see her tears.

"Don't worry, Damion. You don't owe me any explanations." She was impressed with how calm she managed to sound. "You won your bet and gave me a fun time into the bargain. Thanks for a great night. What more could we possibly have to say to each other?"

She closed the bathroom door, locking it behind her, and stepped into the shower, turning the water on full blast and letting the cold spray pound hard on her head. The shock to her system was sufficient to cut off all thought. After five minutes her teeth started to chatter, so she made the water a little hotter. The warmth was relaxing, but unfortunately the power of thought returned along with the rise in temperature.

Her father's words seemed to be etched in acid on her soul. He hadn't been morally outraged to find her in Damion's bed, she thought sadly. He hadn't even been concerned about her doing something that might hurt her emotionally. He had merely been astonished that Damion Tanner—who had his pick of the world's desirable women—should choose to sleep with boring little Alessandra Hawkins. Seeing things from her father's perspective, she could only feel astonishment herself.

Damion had thoughtfully provided shampoo and conditioner, for his guests, along with scented body oil and liquid friction lotion. Nothing but the best for his popsies, she thought cynically. They might enjoy only one night in his arms, but he was determined to make it a night they would remember. Rubbing shampoo fiercely into her hair, she tried to convince herself that the lather was causing her eyes to water.

What had she wanted her father to do? she wondered wryly. Had she hoped he'd seize Damion by the scruff of the neck and demand to know if his intentions were honorable? The thought of her father behaving so conventionally was almost ludicrous enough to make her smile.

The truth was that her father, like the housekeeper, clearly viewed her presence in Damion's bed as a routine episode in Hollywood's ongoing game of musical lovers. She had spent her adult life determined to stay away from the game. If she was hurting now, she had only herself to blame, because she had stepped quite knowingly into the playground. She couldn't blame Damion because she had forgotten the rules and fallen in love with him.

When she reentered the bedroom, wrapped in a towel, no one was in sight. Someone, presumably the housekeeper, had retrieved her clothes from the floor of the den and laid them neatly on the bed. She blushed again, hot and sick with embarrassment at what the housekeeper must have thought as she picked up underclothes, shoes, and pantyhose from all over the fur rugs.

Her hands shook as she sat down in front of the mirror and pulled her hair into the tightest bun possible. Her blouse was missing a couple of buttons toward the waistline, but their absence wouldn't be noticeable if she kept her suit jacket closed. By some miracle her stockings had no runs in them, and she felt reasonably tidy as she tucked her purse under her arm and walked firmly down the hall to the living room. Her pride was hanging in tatters around her, but she was determined to cling to whatever shreds of dignity remained.

The living room door was ajar. She knocked lightly on it and walked in. Her father and Damion were huddled on the sofa, pages of manuscript strewn all over the room.

"I'm just leaving," she said coolly. "I'm planning to

stop at the hospital to see my mother. Do you have any messages for her?"

"Give her my love," Richard said absently. "Glad to know she's doing so well." He shuffled through a pile of pages stacked at his feet. "What the hell did we do with that scene where Judd threatens to kill his wife's lover?"

"It's over here, I think." Damion picked up a slim sheaf of papers from the coffee table. "Yes, this is it. Good scene. Heavy emotional impact."

"Good-bye, Damion," Sandi said.

He looked up dazedly, his eyes scarcely focused. If she hadn't seen the identical expression on her mother's face dozens of times, she would have thought he was high on something.

"Good-bye, honey," he said, his gaze returning almost immediately to the pages in front of him. She had the distinct impression he'd called her honey because he couldn't remember her name. "I'll phone you some time this evening," he added vaguely.

"Of course."

Her irony was entirely wasted, since he gave no impression of having heard her reply. She was downstairs in the lobby before she remembered that her car was still in the parking lot at the clinic, and she had no means of transporting herself across town. The doorman pointed out the pay phone, and she summoned a taxi, refusing to give in to the waves of self-pity threatening to wash over her. She should consider herself lucky she had money to pay for cab fare, she thought with a bracing touch of self-mockery.

She wandered out to the sidewalk. The doorman smiled at her. "It's a beautiful day, isn't it, miss? Not a bit of humidity. Ah, there's nowhere in the world like Los Angeles when the sun decides to shine."

She laughed, biting her lip to cut off a ripple of hysteria. "You're right," she said. "There's absolutely nowhere in the world quite like Los Angeles.

Chapter Eleven

SANDI DIDN'T EXPECT Damion to call her, so she wasn't surprised when Saturday night came and went without a single ring of her telephone. Sunday the phone was similarly silent, and by Sunday evening she had managed to convince herself she would probably live even if he didn't call. She reminded herself that he had demonstrated with humiliating thoroughness that his career was a great deal more important to him than their brief affair. She stood in front of the bedroom mirror, ruthlessly assessing her desirability on a scale of one to ten. She put on mauve heather eyeliner and her new satin teddy, but she still couldn't get past four and a half, so she slammed out of the bedroom in disgust. She wanted men to admire her for her personality, didn't she? So why on earth was she prancing around in her underwear, trying to decide if her breasts were firm enough to allow her to go out without a bra?

She ought to be grateful that Damion hadn't called.

Obviously any attempt to prolong their relationship would only end up causing her phenomenal amounts of pain.

But he did say he loved you, some inner voice protested.

The therapist in her snorted a reply. That, my dear girl, is merely because his lovemaking technique is superb. Men are supposed to murmur words of endearment when they're making love. What did you expect a man like Damion to do? Grunt and make animal noises?

She repeated variations on these excellent arguments with mind-numbing frequency during the sleepless hours of Sunday night. By the time she left to attend Bernard's court hearing on Monday morning, she had finally convinced herself that her father's embarrassing arrival had been a blessing in disguise. The sooner she stopped seeing Damion, the sooner her pain would go away.

The judge agreed to let Bernard off with a fine and probation, so her heart was a little lighter as she returned to the clinic at lunch time. A huge bunch of red roses waited in her office with a large white florist's card attached to the cellophane wrapping. There was no envelope, so the message—in oversized writing—was left plain for everyone to see: "I'm free at seven tonight. My place or yours?" There was no signature.

For about two seconds she couldn't make up her mind whether to scream with rage because of his arrogance or leap with joy because he still wanted her. Fury won out. She'd be damned if she was going to call him back, nor did she have any intention of being home if he happened to stop by her apartment. How dare he leave such a private message exposed to the eyes of the entire world! How dare he assume that there was no need to sign his name! For all he knew she might have a half-dozen lovers vying for her attention.

She rummaged around on her desk until she found an invitation to a professional seminar being held that evening. It happened to be a symposium on premenstrual stress in menopausal women, but she told herself sternly that the information would no doubt be invaluable.

She pressed her intercom. "Glenna, if Mr. Tanner calls, please tell him I'm out of the office."

There was a moment's astonished silence. "But you never lie about where you are, Sandi."

"I'm making a special exception for Mr. Tanner," she said grimly, then shut the intercom off with a decisive click.

Afraid that her resolve might weaken if she went back to her apartment, she drove straight from the clinic to the lecture hall. At the end of the symposium she had no idea whether it had been boring or useful, since she had spent the entire three hours daydreaming about Damion.

Her phone rang five minutes after she got home. "I missed you this evening," Damion said softly. "I've been calling all night long. My bed feels empty without you, and my arms feel even lonelier."

Her heart was pounding loud enough for him to hear clear over the telephone wires. Her bones once again felt like melting Jell-O, and her thought processes weren't in much better shape. She bit her tongue to stop from whispering that she'd missed him, too.

"Peter!" she exclaimed delightedly. "You're back in town! I thought the roses must be from you even though the card wasn't signed."

Damion said something short and crude. "You know damn well this isn't Peter," he said curtly. "Why didn't you answer my invitation, Sandi?"

"Why should I answer such an arrogant message? Why didn't you sign your note? Do you think you're the only man who asks me out?"

"No," he said. "But I hoped I was the only one who was important to you."

Her pent-up breath exploded into the phone. "Like I'm important to *you*, Damion? Like I was so important that for two whole days after the first time we made love you were too busy to call me?"

"Sandi, those were special circumstances. Let me see you and I can explain—"

"I understand already, Damion." The anger drained out of her, leaving her voice flat and weary. "Where movies are concerned, there are *always* special circumstances."

"Don't tell me you never have a crisis in your job. There must be times when the needs of your patients take precedence over everything else. There have to be if you're a competent, caring professional."

"Of course we have crises at the clinic," she agreed. "But they rarely last as long as two days, and they don't occur on a daily basis. The movie industry seems to operate in a continuous, uninterrupted state of crisis."

There was a short pause. "We can't talk on the phone, Sandi. We have too many misunderstandings to clear up. Will you be home tomorrow evening?"

Her emotions urged her to say she would always be home for him, but her mind was marginally more practical. After a single night of Damion's lovemaking she was dying inside. What would happen if she allowed the relationship to continue? How would she survive the inevitable separation if she let herself depend on him?

"No, Damion," she said firmly. "I'm not going to be home tomorrow evening."

She hung up the phone, then dialed a forwarding code so that all calls would go to her answering service. She then proceeded to prove exactly how sensible she was by crying for a solid hour until she finally fell asleep.

Sandi was thrilled when Gabriella Barini left the hospital right on schedule and installed herself, with considerable fanfare, in her favorite suite at the Bel Air Hotel. Four nurses and two aides worked in seven-hour shifts so she would never lack the attention she needed, and her convalescence progressed rapidly. Her radiant beauty soon returned, although she still hadn't fully recovered her physical strength.

Soon after her release from the hospital, she invited Sandi to dinner in her suite. There was no point in going out, she said, when she wasn't allowed to eat anything that tasted like real food. Sandi, who scarcely noticed what went into her mouth these days, listlessly agreed that the room service menu would be fine.

Gabriella ordered poached chicken breasts, steamed rice, and pureed carrots. Sandi, lacking the energy to make a different choice, ordered the same.

"Baby food." Gabriella snorted disgustedly when their meal arrived. She picked up her fork and took a mouthful of chicken, avoiding her daughter's eyes. Sandi had the extraordinary impression that her mother—who was surely one of the world's most self-assured women— wasn't entirely at her ease.

"Damion Tanner came to see me this afternoon," she said abruptly.

Much to her annoyance, Sandi felt her cheeks grow hot. It seemed like months since she'd seen him, and her knees still shook every time somebody mentioned his name.

She reached for a bread stick and crunched down hard. "Did he?" she said in a valiant attempt to sound casual. "How nice for you. Has his new movie gone into production yet?"

"I have no idea. I know the schedule of my own movie, and that is more than enough." Gabriella sipped from a glass of water, and Sandi waited impatiently for her to continue. She wasn't hungry for food, but she was starving for news of Damion.

"I like your new hairstyle," Gabriella said, to Sandi's intense frustration. "It's soft, yet still suitable for the classic purity of your features. Your dress, too, is very attractive. That delicate shade of mauve is flattering to your eyes and to your complexion."

"Is it?" Sandi got up from the table and walked agitatedly around the room. "I'm glad you like my dress," she said. "I decided my wardrobe could use some brightening up."

"For once our opinions are in total harmony," Gabriella said dryly.

Sandi pulled her napkin through her fingers, then realized what she was doing and tossed it onto her chair. "Did—um—did Damion say anything interesting when he was with you this afternoon?"

"Why, of course he did! What an odd question. Damion is a most entertaining conversationalist."

"Did he . . . did he say anything about me?" Sandi asked doggedly, feeling her face and neck flame with heat.

"I'm sure he must have," Gabriella remarked. "It would be odd if he visited me and did not mention your name. Tell me, what do you think of this negligee I am wearing? It is an intriguing shade of blue, is it not? I was wondering if I should have a dress made up in the same color."

"It's a wonderful shade of blue," Sandi said, sitting down in her chair with a dispirited thump. "But you always look wonderful in blue. You look wonderful in everything."

Gabriella glanced at her daughter, a faint smile curving her lips. "That, my dear child, is where you are wrong. There are a multitude of designs and colors in which I look terrible. It is merely that I am sensible enough never to wear something that does not flatter me."

"You're not sensible at all," Sandi said gloomily. "I'm the one who's sensible in our family."

"And that, my dear, is definitely a matter of opinion. By the way, I have been asked to appear on Mark Kline's television program on Wednesday morning. You really must watch the show."

Sandi looked up, somewhat surprised by her mother's

news. "You don't usually enjoy doing live television. Are you certain you'll be well enough?"

"I'm certain." Gabriella smiled again. She had finished her dinner and looked uncommonly pleased with herself. "Would you like some dessert?" she asked.

"Yes," Sandi said recklessly, not caring that her mother would inevitably deliver a twenty-minute lecture on the evils of butter fat and sugar. "I'd like a chocolate fudge sundae with whipped cream and extra nuts."

"Certainly you must have one," Gabriella said. "Although personally I have never found chocolate to be any use whatsoever in easing the pain of a broken heart."

Sandi walked over to the telephone and silently dialed room service. She was wise enough not to ask what her mother was talking about.

Sandi was eating breakfast on Wednesday when she remembered that her mother was scheduled to appear on Mark Kline's television show. She picked up her coffee, walked through to the living room, and flipped on the set. Seven forty-five. The show had already been on the air for fifteen minutes.

"Welcome back." Mark Kline's handsome features smiled into her living room. "We are fortunate to have a great actress and a world-renowned movie star with us this morning. Gabriella Barini has recently recovered from minor surgery and will be starting work on her latest movie next week." Mark Kline turned to his guest, and the camera panned in on Gabriella's exquisite, glowing features. "Tell us about your new movie," he said. "I understand there will be some unusual features in the role you're playing."

Gabriella flashed him one of her most dazzling smiles. "It is true that my movie is very exciting," she said. Even over the airwaves her voice throbbed with the promise of passion. Unlike some movie stars she was adept at handling interviews. "But this morning I am too happy to talk about my professional plans. Today I talk as a mother." Her eyelashes fluttered, and Gabriella miraculously transformed herself into a perfect illusion of maternal pride.

As she stared at the screen, Sandi felt her stomach lurch with a premonition of impending disaster.

"I talk of my daughter Alessandra Hawkins, the child of my marriage to Richard Hawkins." Gabriella lowered her voice confidingly. Her warm manner invited ten million television viewers to share in her family secrets. "In some ways, I am still a typical mother at heart, and an old-fashioned one at that. So you can imagine the pleasure I have in announcing that my dear daughter is about to be married."

"Married!" Mark Kline exclaimed. It was clear that this interview was not going according to plan.

Sandi sank down into the nearest armchair. Somehow, looking at her mother's self-satisfied expression, she had a dreadful feeling that the worst was yet to come.

"Yes." Gabriella gave vent to a sentimental sigh. "My daughter is to marry Damion Tanner next week. They are very much in love, you understand. It is so touching to watch them when they are together."

Sandi put both hands around her coffee cup, then leaned forward with extreme care to put the cup down on the table. Once she had accomplished that small task, she jumped to her feet and began to yell wildly at her TV screen.

"Have you gone crazy?" she screamed at her mother. "Did Dr. Matthews take out a piece of your brain as well as your gallbladder? How could you do this to me? How could you be so *cruel!*"

She realized she was so busy screaming that she had missed at least three of Mark Kline's questions. She quieted down just in time to hear her mother say that, although the wedding ceremony was to be private, the arrangements had all been made, and "dear Alessandra" was planning to purchase her wedding gown that very afternoon. "Dear Alessandra," according to Gabriella, was planning to wear the traditional white and would carry pale pink rosebuds.

"My daughter is very conservative, you understand," Gabriella murmured. "She wishes everything about her marriage to be traditional. For her there will be only one love in her life, and I am deeply happy that she has found it with such an exciting, interesting man."

There was a red haze in front of Sandi's eyes as she stormed over and punched off the television set. She wouldn't have been answerable for the consequences if she had listened to any more of her mother's extraordinary lies. She spent a blissful five minutes trying to decide whether to boil her mother in oil or expose her to ravenous wolves, then marched into the kitchen and poured herself a large glass of water. She gulped it down without pausing for breath.

The phone started to ring, but she made no attempt to pick it up. She didn't trust herself to be coherent, much less polite. She went into her bedroom and stripped off all her clothes, then remembered she was supposed to be on her way to work and pulled them all on again. She was struggling with a twisted pair of pantyhose when her anger finally cooled sufficiently for her to think straight.

Why was she so furious with her mother? Bewilderment, or at worst mild annoyance, would surely be a more appropriate reaction. After all, Gabriella's announcement had done no permanent harm. True, there would be no point in denying Gabriella's story; reporters would simply assume she was trying to keep the exact time and place of her wedding secret. But she had plenty of experience in sending determined reporters off the track, and she knew she could kill the story if she set her mind to it. One of the minor blessings of the Hollywood gossip machine was that it chewed over only the latest and hottest news items. A failed love affair was even less newsworthy than one that hadn't started.

Her anger had a more subtle cause, she admitted sadly. She was furious because she wished so desperately that Gabriella's claims were true.

Sandi removed all the pins from her hair and started to brush it, then realized she'd already done her hair once that morning. The task of restyling it suddenly seemed unbearably burdensome. She stood at the dressing table, paralyzed by an aching sensation of loss.

She heard the buzz of the doorbell and moved automatically to open the door, then registered that the last thing in the world she wanted at this moment was to entertain visitors. In the act of reaching for the chain her hand fell back to her side.

The doorbell rang again. "Sandi, open this damn door! Right now!"

She swallowed hard. "I can't. I'm not here."

"That's good," he said smoothly. "That means you won't get hurt when I break down the door."

"You can't do that, Damion!"

"Watch me," he said tersely.

She didn't stop to reflect that the door was solid oak, reinforced with steel. Damion sounded determined enough to find an ax. She opened the door.

He was wearing faded jeans, scuffed loafers, and a baggy, ill-fitting cotton sweater. Sandi thought he had never looked more desirable. His eyes were bright with temper, and his body was hard with tension. He strode into her living room, anger creating an almost visible aura around him. She wanted to be swept into his arms so badly that she could almost taste it.

"What the hell are you and Gabriella up to?" he demanded, pacing up and down the living room. "You refuse to see me or speak to me for more than a week, and then I—along with a few million other people— suddenly hear that we're planning to get married! Did you even think of asking my opinion about all this? Or were you planning to shanghai me and drag me to the altar?"

She turned away from him, forcing herself to feel anger. It was, she thought bleakly, slightly more dignified than bursting into tears and begging him to kiss her.

"I'm not up to anything," she said tightly. "Do you think I *wanted* my mother to go on the air and make a stupid, ridiculous announcement like that?"

He stopped in midstride. "What's so ridiculous about it? Incredible as it may seem to you, there have been several women in my life who would have *liked* to marry me!"

"That doesn't seem incredible," she said cuttingly. "The movie industry is notorious for attracting masochists!"

They had been moving steadily closer, and now they stood only inches apart. Feeling the heat of his body radiating across the tiny space that separated them, she closed her eyes, willing herself not to cross the fragile barrier that kept her safe.

"Sandi . . ."

She heard the tenderness of his voice and clutched her arms around her waist in a final, desperate gesture of self-defense.

"Look, I'm sorry, Damion. I really didn't know what my mother was planning to do. I'll notify the press right away and let them know it was all a mistake."

"Sandi," he said quietly, "please look at me."

His breath was warm on her cheek, and even though her eyes were closed, she knew he was leaning toward her. In just a minute, if she didn't move, he would kiss her. Surely one kiss wouldn't matter too much . . .

They both jumped like startled rabbits when the doorbell buzzed, long and imperiously.

Sandi snapped out of her trance and tottered to the door, just enough in command of herself to inquire who was there.

"It is I!" Gabriella proclaimed. Even through two inches

of oak and steel Sandi could tell that her mother was thoroughly pleased with herself.

Sandi tore open the door, but before she could let loose a volley of outraged questions, Gabriella slipped past and floated into the living room. A cloud of her favorite perfume settled over the little hallway.

Sandi trailed behind her mother into the living room, where Damion was pacing like a ferocious caged tiger. Gabriella greeted him with a benign, maternal smile.

"Dear boy," she said. "How fortunate that you are here already! We can make all our explanations together."

"I don't feel *I* have any explanations to make," Damion said, his voice exceptionally dry.

"Do you mean you have already told Sandi how much you love her? That is very good. Such an explanation will save us all a great deal of time."

For once in his life Damion seemed at a total loss for words. Sandi abandoned her effort to remain standing and sank bonelessly onto the sofa. When her mother threw herself into a new role, Sandi reflected resignedly, she certainly pulled out all the stops. At that moment Gabriella was standing regally in the middle of the room, giving a brilliant imitation of Queen Elizabeth welcoming Princess Diana into the Royal Family.

"You are both very quiet this morning," Gabriella said. She gave another indulgent smile as she extended her hands toward Damion.

He obediently bowed over them and escorted her to a chair. She seated herself with a gracious nod, arranging her silk dress in an elegant swirl around her knees.

"Well, now," she said. "It will be simplest, I believe, if you two do not talk. You have neither of you made much sense recently, so it is unlikely you will have anything useful to contribute to our discussion."

Sandi finally recovered the use of her voice. "Hold on a minute, Mother! You're not going to steamroll us that easily. Damion and I would both like an explanation for the crazy announcement you made on Mark Kline's

ogram. How could you possibly do something so ir-
sponsible?"

Her mother's exquisite features betrayed absolutely
no sign of guilt or embarrassment. "There was nothing
ridiculous about my announcement," she said tartly. "Even
your father said it was an excellent plan. An ideal solution
to an impossible situation."

"If you and Dad are in agreement about something,
that proves it was totally crazy," Sandi muttered.

Gabriella frowned disapprovingly. "My dear child, it
has been plain to everybody that you and Damion are
making yourselves hopelessly miserable by staying apart.
However, you are both too stubborn to admit how you
feel for each other, so we decided that I should bring
you together again. As Richard said, if the pair of you
are determined to be miserable, you may as well be
miserable together. Personally I do not approve of marriage, which is a very boring institution, but you and
Damion share these strange ideas about loyalty and faith-
fulness and living together until the end of your lives.
Richard and I have decided you are ideally suited to each
other."

Gabriella paused as if to contemplate the full oddity
of wanting to remain married to the same person for an
entire lifetime. The concept was obviously too bewil-
dering for her to grasp, and she shrugged.

"Richard thinks you had better get married as soon as
possible. He claims that Damion hasn't turned in a useful day's work since he met you."

Sandi spoke through gritted teeth. "I will *not* marry
Damion in order to improve the work schedule on my
father's next movie."

"Certainly not," Gabriella said. "You will marry him
because you love him." She stood up, smoothing the
delicate pleats of her dress. "Your father and I are both
frantically busy, but we have set aside next Thursday to
attend your wedding."

Damion looked searchingly at Gabriella. "Why do you

think Sandi is in love with me?" he asked tersely.

"Because she is my daughter," Gabriella said, producing another infuriatingly superior smile. "But if you doubt my judgment, Damion, ask her yourself. Perhaps she will surprise you with her answer."

She walked gracefully toward the door. "It is time for me to go. Richard has sent his limousine for me. We are to eat lunch together while we discuss the best place for the ceremony. Naturally we do not want your wedding day to be ruined by mobs of reporters. We thought, Richard and I, that you would prefer a private ceremony."

Sandi jumped up from the sofa. "For the last time, Mother, there isn't going to be a wedding! Damion and I have absolutely nothing in common. Nothing!"

"That is not quite what your father told me," Gabriella said. "And, like your father, I do not think you would go to bed with a man for whom you feel nothing."

As deathly silence filled the room, Gabriella paused in the doorway, one hand resting stylishly against the frame, the other holding her purse at the perfect angle for a camera. She had always been marvelous at making dramatic exits.

"When I was in the hospital, there was much time for reflection and I have decided that I am no longer going to be a young woman. Now that it is fashionable to be forty, I plan to stun the world with my mature beauty and my thoughtful insights into the world condition."

"That's an excellent idea, Mother—"

"Naturally it is an excellent idea," Gabriella interrupted. "My ideas are invariably brilliant. However, I have decided that I need a grandchild to hold in next year's studio publicity shots, and we do not have any time to waste if you are to produce my grandchild on schedule. It will be a very effective picture, don't you think? I will probably wear something blue, and the baby can wear cream. Cream is a good color for babies, especially if they are red and wrinkled."

Sandi's mouth was gaping open, and she didn't dare nce at Damion. She cut off an exasperated snort, not te sure whether she wanted to burst out laughing or olve into floods of tears. She was quite certain, however, that she wanted to murder her mother.

iella flashed one final, all-encompassing smile, the fact that they both appeared rooted to the

o, please, do not bother to show me out. You have much to say to each other. Oh, by the way, Sandi, I informed your secretary yesterday that you would not be in today. She has rescheduled your patients accordingly."

Gabriella opened the front door with uncharacteristic briskness and let herself out, leaving Damion and Sandi alone in the living room, staring at each other in uncomfortable silence.

Nervously Sandi pushed a strand of hair behind her ear. "It would never work, you know," she said finally.

"What would never work? Allowing our child to appear in Gabriella's publicity photos?"

Sandi gave a reluctant smile. "No, I'm sure that would work wonderfully. My mother's instincts for publicity are infallible. And she's quite right; over forty is suddenly the age to be."

There was another short silence. "Why wouldn't you see me?" Damion asked abruptly. "Why wouldn't you answer my calls? Dammit, Sandi, when we made love that night, didn't it mean anything to you?"

Too much, she thought. *Too dangerously much.* She stared down at the pale gray carpet as if she had never seen it before. "Damion, I . . . care for you, and I'm . . . I'm very attracted to you physically, but I'm scared to let our relationship develop any further." She twisted her hands into a tight knot, then saw what she'd done and carefully untwisted them again. "You could hurt me very badly," she admitted huskily.

Long before she had finished speaking she was in his

arms, her stomach pressed hard against him as his han
caressed her spine.

"How can you imagine that I would hurt you? Swe
heart, there's nothing in the world I want more than
love you."

"Maybe that's true today," she said sadly, "but a
marriage needs more than two people who think
in love. I've grown up seeing this week's love a
the century turn into next week's divorce case spe
ular." Her voice died away to little more than a whisp
"Damion, I couldn't bear it if I let myself love you. It
would hurt too much when you left me."

His hands stroked gently over the curve of her hips,
molding her tightly against his body. "I'm not going to
leave you, Sandi. It's taken me thirty-three years to find
you, and I'm not about to let you go." He cupped her
face, gazing searchingly into her eyes. "Don't confuse
me with your parents, Sandi. Your mother and father live
their publicity. I have a PR agent who creates mine. We're
in the same profession, your parents and I, but our values
and our lifestyles are utterly different."

"That's true in some ways, but not in others. Your
profession comes first with you, Damion. It always has."

"Acting's important to me," he admitted. "Vitally important. But your work is important to you, too, so you
should understand how I feel. When Bernard approached
you in the parking lot outside the clinic, you scarcely
even remembered I was there. For a little while you were
totally absorbed in his problems. Don't misunderstand—
I'm not complaining. That's how I think it should be."

"Am I supposed to be reassured?" she asked wryly.
"You mean because we're both workaholics, somehow
a long-term relationship between us is going to work
out?"

"No," he said quietly. "I guess I mean that in the past
my career was more important to me than anything else.
But that was before I met you." A flicker of intense

otion crossed his face. "I love you too much to let
career or anything else come between us, Sandi. I'm
going to allow you to create obstacles where none
ts. If you love me, we can find some way to cope
the demands of our careers."

skimmed his hair with trembling fingers, not trust-
lf to touch him more intimately. "Maybe you
t me physically."

mouth twisted wryly. "Honey, I sure do want you
ically, but I have years of experience in desiring a
man's body and, believe me, what I feel for you bears
o resemblance to something nice and comfortable like
a simple desire for sex."

He twined his hands into the long strands of her hair,
and his thumbs gently caressed the sensitive skin behind
her ears. As her body trembled on the brink of submission, she fought against the temptation to close her eyes
and surrender to the magic of his touch. She searched
despairingly for the words that would make him understand why she couldn't just fall into his arms and count
the world well lost for love.

"Damion, making love with you was one of the most
beautiful experiences of my life. I hoped maybe it was
special for you, too. But when my father came to your
apartment, he only had to mention that script option and
you forgot all about me." Feeling tears gather at the
ners of her eyes, she dashed them away.

"Damion, we're not just talking about two people with
conflicting career schedules. I grew up taking second
place to my parents' professions. I couldn't bear to take
second place in your life as well." Her voice died away.
"The problem is . . . I love you too much to play second
fiddle to a script option."

He rocked her gently in his arms, then guided her
over to the sofa and pulled her onto his lap. "I know my
behavior must have seemed pretty insensitive," he said
quietly. "But I was feeling guilty as hell. In the first place

it was extremely disconcerting to wake up and find
self eyeball to eyeball with your father. Even a confirm
superstud finds it a bit difficult to sweep a woman i
his arms and whisper sweet nothings when her fath
standing glowering at the end of the bed."

She managed a faint smile. "You've never had to
with a glowering father before, huh?"

He grinned. "Thank God, no! Last Saturda
first. But even if Richard hadn't found you in m
he had every right to be angry. The script he can
discuss had been sitting on my desk for ages, and I had
even glanced at the title page—chiefly because I'd bee
too damn busy mooning over you. The studio invested
hundreds of thousands of dollars so that your father and
I could have the first option on that screenplay. I had an
absolute obligation to decide before the deadline whether
or not they should put up another half-million dollars to
buy the film rights."

Her fingers plucked nervously at a loose thread in a
sofa cushion. "I've always made important decisions logically, Damion, but I can't seem to do that when we're
together. I've always been the one who stayed calm and
in control, but with you, I never feel calm. Sometimes
you only have to look at me and my body starts to leap
out of control." Her eyes were troubled as she gazed at
him. "I don't know how to handle those feelings. They
frighten me."

His eyes glowed with mischief. "Honey, that's pr
ably the best news I've heard so far today. What's more
I have the perfect answer to your problem. If you'll take
me to your bedroom, I'll demonstrate the most marvelous
cure for what ails you, and I promise it won't hurt a bit."

She couldn't help smiling. "You make it all sound so
simple."

"That's because it *is* simple. Only a doctor of psychology specializing in sex therapy would make it seem
complicated."

He began to unfasten her blouse, planting a delicate
w of kisses against her breasts as he opened each but-
on.

"This is the first stage of the cure," he said as he
ched the final button. "What do you think of it so

drew in a shaky breath. "Interesting."

gets better," he said, adjusting her position on his
aking her instantly aware that she wasn't the only
who had been aroused. Instinctively she arched her
ack against his arms. He cupped her breasts in his hands,
all laughter dying from his face.

"I love you, Sandi," he breathed. "It's never been like
this for me with anybody else. Sometimes during the past
week I thought I'd go crazy from wanting you."

Something painful that had spent a lifetime coiled deep
and tight inside her suddenly snapped, and she gave a
tiny sigh of liberation as she leaned her head against his
chest.

"I love you, too, Damion," she said, feeling a rush
of joy as she made the confession. "I just never knew
that loving somebody would feel this . . . this *disorgan-
ized.*"

Her body shook in his embrace, but she realized that
it didn't matter if he sensed her passion or her confusion.
h Damion she didn't have to mask her emotions. She
n't always have to be strong and calm and disciplined
nd in control. He loved her, and that meant that with
him she could just be herself.

His heart pounded erratically against her cheek as he
swept her up from the sofa and paused at the living room
door. "I was planning to carry you off to the nearest
bed," he said, his smile tender as he looked down at her,
"but I just remembered I don't know where your bedroom
is."

"First door on the right," she murmured.

He strode confidently down the hallway and pushed

the door open with his shoulder in time-honored movi
star fashion. Once inside the room, however, he halte
abruptly.

"Well, well, well," he murmured. "What a *very* i
teresting room."

Too late, she remembered that nobody was eve
lowed in her bedroom. At first glance the deco
seem different from that of the rest of the apartmer
walls were stark white, the carpeting gray, and the
dows covered with practical venetian blinds. The re
was a cool, uncluttered appearance that enhanced th
image she had spent most of her lifetime projecting.

Damion, however, wasn't looking at the walls, the
blinds, or the carpeting. He wasn't even looking at the
vase on her dressing table that held a dozen drooping red
roses. He was looking at the only picture in the room,
a poster hung centrally and conspicuously over her austere twin bed.

He examined the poster in silence for a couple of
seconds, then kissed her gently on the tip of the nose.
"I like your taste in art," he said, and there was no
mockery in his voice, only love and a hint of affectionate
laughter.

Resolutely she kept her gaze turned away from the
picture, a life-size photograph of Damion Tanner, stripped
for action in the final love scene of *A Dream of Darkn*

"My father happened to have an extra poster in
office," she mumbled. "It seemed a waste to throw
away."

"Sure," he said. "Gee, it's good to know I'm going
to marry somebody so thrifty."

He carried her over to the bed, eased her to her feet,
and stripped off the severe gray and white bedspread
before she gathered wits enough to stop him. His entire
body shook with laughter when he saw the flaming red
satin sheets.

He pushed her gently down on the bed and lay beside